Like A Fish Understands A Tree

Helen Collins

Published by
Paradigm Consultancy & Development Agency Ltd

Printed by
Colour Jay Ltd

Proof reading by
Amanda Jones Editorial Services

ISBN: 0-9543068-3-X

Written by Helen Collins

Paradigm
8 Brandon Street
Birkenhead
CH41 5HN
Tel: 0870 010 4933
Fax: 0870 010 4934
Email: admin@paradigm-uk.org

www.paradigm-uk.org

Thanks to . . .

Mark Michalowski, for starting it all with an email about a creative writing competition, National Novel Writing Month (www.nanowrimo.org).

Weekly emails from **Chris Batty** from nanowrimo kept me on track during November 2003, when the first draft was written.

The 'first draft' reading group – **Dave Edwards, Jo Blackburn, Gail Emo, Maggie Moon, and Frances Burditt** (hi mum). Without your support and encouragement this would have gone no further.

Everyone who has read it since and offered feedback, in particular **Robert Evans, Harvey Huckerby, Jane Hobson** and **The Pendeen Reading Group.**

To **Joe Hutchinson** for wanting a mention.

Huge thanks specifically to **Simon Duffy** for all your support, enthusiasm and unwavering belief in me.

Everyone else at Paradigm; Peter, Nigel, Judith, Nicola, Kathy, Ellen, Suzanne, Wendy and Pam.

Thanks to **Dave Hingsburger** for loving the book, offering fantastic feedback and for the beautiful 'outro'.

Finally for ongoing encouragement, endlessly cooking while I'm typing, listening to me ramble on into the small hours, for all the commas and for always being there, **Norma.**

For Norma

Chapter 1

Peter was falling. He was in a narrow, vertical tunnel, like a mine shaft and he was falling. He was falling very quickly – too fast, he thought, to survive landing. There was no sign of any end to it. Having worked out what was happening he realised that the air rushing past his ears and the movement of his body through the air was distracting him from thinking clearly. Better to stop falling.

He calmly felt under his leather tunic and reached into a pocket in his belt. He brought out a small heavy metal cylinder. Holding it horizontally across his chest he braced himself and shook the cylinder firmly once. Peter was not entirely sure what would happen, but as this was the only equipment he had on him, it was the only thing he could do. In fact exactly what he hoped would happen did – the tube expanded instantly from both ends, hit the sides of the tunnel and dragged in the rock on each side until both ends found secure purchase on each side of the tunnel wall, at which point he stopped falling.

Or at least, the c-cylinder stopped falling. Peter would only stop if he managed to keep hold of it. As the tube expanded two rubberised handgrips appeared a body width apart along its smooth, steel surface. Peter's only chance to stop falling, and keep his c-cylinder, was to get his hands onto these grips before it got stuck into the rock. He managed it, but only just. He hung, swinging slightly, the metal rod high above his head, his feet dangling into the blackness below. Hmmm.

Now what?

He caught his breath, took a moment to thank something or other for the couple of seconds drag on the rock, which gave him time to find the hand holds and slowed him down slightly. He had not fully thought through what would happen. Although the stick stopped, his body had carried on falling at the same rate. His wrists and shoulders were burning from the wrench.

After a short rest he swung himself backwards and forwards a couple of times before using the momentum to help pull himself up, hooking a knee round the pole and hauling himself up to a precarious sitting position. He inched gingerly to his left until he could feel the rock. There was a dull greenish light coming from it and he could just make out the scar his c-cylinder had cut into the surface. He let his fingers travel over the mark and the rock. Looking up he could see nothing but the walls of this vertical cave, looking down looked exactly the same. His head swam and he stared straight ahead for a moment to get his bearings again and be sure of which way was up.

About four minutes later, after an exhaustive investigation of his situation and surroundings Peter was coming to the reluctant conclusion that there was nothing he could do here. He was stuck. The only thing he could possibly do was retract the c-cylinder and carry on falling. There was nothing on the walls on either side, no switches, secret passages or anything. He figured the chances of actually getting the damn thing to stop him in exactly the right place to find anything like that were so small that he was sure it was not what he was supposed to do. He sighed a deep sigh, held his breath, and pressed the button which retracted the stick.

Peter was falling. He breathed out, put the c-cylinder away and immediately landed. He realised that he could not have been very far from the bottom when he stopped. He landed well, knees bent slightly and ready to roll. Roll where exactly he was not sure, unless there was going to be an opening of some sort. He guessed there must be something down there for him and he was right. There was, in fact, a cave. It was tall enough for a man to walk down, still heading downhill. Peter had braced himself to land and roll, so roll he did. He somehow managed to roll right into the opening of this cave, and he carried on rolling. He simply, helplessly rolled, bumping into the sides. He was confused and disorientated, unable to stop himself.

It seemed like forever before the gradient changed and he slowed to a flapping stop, legs and arms splayed out and heart racing at an alarming rate. He lay still. With his heartbeat like that there was nothing else to do for a minute. He lay and listened to the beating gently slow to something less alarming. Then he got himself up, shook himself down and checked for damage. He was filthy, his tunic was torn, and he had some damage to his wrists, shoulders and a couple of fingers. The c-cylinder was fine and worked perfectly. Peter was amazed to find he still had all his water, food and first aid kit. Excellent. After applying first aid to his damaged areas he stood up, breathed in, and walked forward into the cave; he had made it, he was in, and Peter was ready to begin.

*   *   *

Susan sat staring out of the window, her chin in her hand, and elbow on the desk, eyes glazed. She was thinking . . . that was clear, but probably not about the lesson. Mr Sullivan stopped talking and walked quietly over to her seat. She took no notice at all. This proved to him she had been not been paying attention. He had been talking, and all the other kids were looking at him now. Even those whose minds had drifted off slightly had been roused by the silence. But not Susan. No, she was off on some journey somewhere in her head, barely conscious that she was in school, let alone in a very interesting lesson that he was in the process of explaining. Reaching her desk, he placed his hands carefully behind his back. He always did this now; he noticed most of the teachers did it when they were close to a student. If he placed his hands deliberately behind his back then it sent a clear signal that he could not at any time have touched the student. It was self-protection. His hands clasped at the base of his spine he leaned in towards Susan, raised his voice and carried on talking where he had left off,

"It is clear to see from this whole story that the test here was not whether he would kill his own son, but whether he would in fact do anything God asked him to. It was intended only to test Abraham's faith."

Mr Sullivan turned away from Susan almost as soon as he had started speaking. She had jumped visibly and turned a darker shade of crimson. He was satisfied that he had her attention, he hoped she did not get too much stick from the other kids after class. Spreading his arms wide Mr Sullivan spun to include the whole class as he continued round the room.

"Now, the interesting thing for me in this passage is how it changed God in my view – my opinion of God was altered irrevocably after reading this one story. Was he doing it just to flex his muscles? Just to see how much power he had over humans? When I was your age and read this passage, I hated God for doing this. Now, of course, I know that this was in fact the start of the Jewish faith. It was an illustration to show non-believers that here, finally, is a God, a one true God, who did not want animal or human sacrifice. As all other major religions had some form of sacrificial 'giving of life' to the gods, this story is used to illustrate how the One God is different. Although I understand that now, I still read it and feel anger at God for his manipulation of Abraham."

Mr Sullivan carried on, explaining his view that God was, as far as Susan could make out, just an insecure big tease. He went to great lengths to always make it clear that this was his own personal opinion. He had really made her jump and now she was trying to cover up and pretend that she had been paying attention all the time. Had everyone seen her? Susan had learned the best thing to do no matter how bad it looked was to deny it. If you deny everything consistently and for long enough it will all go away and stop happening.

She was not sure if she had imagined Mr Sullivan's voice had suddenly got amazingly loud in her ear, or if he had really come right up to her in front of the whole class. It did not seem likely that Mr Sullivan would do that to her. She could not really remember him being very close, only that he had been walking around the class. Mind you, she had been pretty out of it all right. He could have put a bomb under her and she would not have noticed. It was strange this ability to actually drift off to sleep without having to close her eyes. It added a whole new meaning to the term 'daydreaming'. She had, in fact, been asleep and Mr Sullivan had, in fact, woken her up. She was disorientated and felt dishevelled, at least on the inside. She tried to maintain a calm exterior and to pay attention to what he was saying. Susan had learned the hard way to listen to at least the last ten minutes of any lesson.

Susan was invariably woken by the ringing of the bell at the end of each class, when teachers gave out the homework. Mr Sullivan never made any reference to the contents of the lesson after the bell had rung. He would say, "Homework: write a 2,000 word essay on the future lives of the characters we have been discussing. Class dismissed" or "Homework: Write a 2,000 word essay on your own thoughts and feelings about one of the main characters. Class dismissed". Always the same. Susan had realised after a couple of classes at this school that this was a common trait amongst the teachers here. It meant that if she slept right up to the bell, she had no idea what the homework was supposed to be about. To save any embarrassing conversations in the yard she had to listen before the bell rang. In general it seemed OK to ask fellow students what they thought about the lesson, or which character they were going to write about, but they were all onto her now, and no one would help her out any more.

To start with some of the more helpful girls had tried to explain classes to her. When this had taken more of their time than they wanted to give to a new girl, and she had still not got it, they gave up and left her to it. In her old school it had been cool to doss around and not do very much. Here, if there was a cool gang, they never actually attended any classes and Susan had not seen them. Here everyone was clever and paid attention. Here it was cool to do well and suck up to the damn teachers. Susan was lost. Both inside and out. The place was huge, and she had been here 7 months now and made no friends.

She hated everyone, but especially she hated Mum and Dad for making her come here. Susan knew this was not quite true. She knew that she actually quite liked Mr Sullivan, but she would never admit it, not even to herself. Besides, it sounded better to say she hated everyone, more rebellious and cool. She wished there were other students who felt like this; hell, even one other student would be fun, but that did not quite fit with hating absolutely everyone, so she stuck to it and sulked all the time.

Susan had been sulking with everyone for so long now that she was not sure how to be nice to anyone. Not that she had forgotten, but that she was not sure how to go from sulking to being nice without losing face, or a big fuss being made.

It had been bad enough when she had gone home and talked about Mr Sullivan. It was not his radical religious stance that had upset her parents. She only told them what he had said because she thought that they would remove her from the school if they knew she was being taught such sacrilegious views. But no, her dumb parents had not paid any attention to what Mr Sullivan had actually said at all. No, all they were interested in was that she had talked about an adult without slagging him off.

"I think she likes him better than either of us, Adam, I really do. Have you heard this? She likes him, oh yes, Mr Sotherby this, Mr Sotherby that . . . "

"It's Mr Sullivan, Mum," Susan corrected her.

At this her mother had snapped at her. She could never tell if it was real anger or just put on.

"Oh I see . . . that's important is it, Susan? Important to you that I get his name right? I see . . . you wouldn't care if Adam and I were called Mr and Mrs Bucket, but for Mr Sour-face it's important to you is it? Finally found another human being you give a toss about have you, Susan? Well congratubloodylations!"

Susan had gone upstairs without another word. What was the point? And who cared if Mum was really angry, or just putting it on because she thought that shouting was what she was supposed to do. It still felt like being yelled at for no reason. And clearly they did not care about her enough to worry whether she became a devil-worshipping-heathen-witch so what the hell. It was a dumb way to get out of school anyway.

That had been a few weeks ago now. Susan was finding that she was not sure how to be nice to people. Everyone expected her to be a bitch. She felt this was right and another reason to carry on sulking too, but there were also some times when she would have liked to have been nice, but felt like she could not do it any more. It would make her into a different person or something.

Like with her brother George. Susan liked George a lot, and they had always got on well. She did not want to lose the relationship with him, so instead she was really nice to him in private, when they were on their own, but then horrible to him when anyone else was around. She secretly willed him to understand that she just could not be nice to him when people could see. She knew he did not of course; he was clearly hurt and confused. She did not know what to do.

*   *   *

Sitting and looking at magazines was not George's idea of fun at all. Maybe as a pastime, to have a break in an otherwise busy day, like Mum did, but not as an occupation. Not as your activity for the day. What did they think was in a magazine? More to the point, what did they think was in a magazine for someone who could not read?

George had a timetable in his pocket for what he did every day of the week. For Tuesday morning it had the letters 'M-A-G-A-Z-I-N-E-S' written on it. It had a cut-out picture of a magazine next to it. George hated Tuesdays for this reason. He hated Thursdays as well; Thursday afternoon had the letters 'J-I-G-S-A-W', with a hand-drawn jigsaw piece next to it. For the life of him George did not know what good this was going to do him. He had been asked what he wanted to do and he had said a number of times now that he wanted to cook. Secretly George wanted to be a chef on the TV, chopping and stirring and tasting and above all talking. Constantly talking about food and how much he loved it.

George loved Mondays and Wednesdays. His timetable said 'C-O-L-L-E-G-E' and had a picture of a building on it. This picture said nothing to George about why he loved it. His affection had nothing to do with the building at all; it was the kitchens inside the building that he loved. He had asked whether the picture could be of the kitchen but had been told that as he went to more than just the cookery class it would be more useful to have a picture of the building. George shrugged. George shrugged a lot. He also sighed and nodded a lot. It did not seem to be worth the effort to try and explain that he did not want a picture of the classroom but of the big canteen kitchen. Or that he did not want it there so that he would know what the word COLLEGE meant, but because then he would have a picture of the kitchen, that he could carry around with him and look at it whenever he wanted to. Instead he shrugged and said nothing.

George did not really talk very much at the centre any more; he had learned over the years that there was no point. It took George a while to hear the words people said to him, and not many people had the patience to wait for him to answer. Everyone who went to the centre had a learning disability. The place had been built in the 1960s on an industrial site to provide work for disabled people. It was built to look and function like a factory, with some large warehouse work areas and some smaller, educational rooms.

Now, well past the turn of the century, there were still a hundred people who turned up every day, but there was no work for them to do any more. The more modern approach was to provide 'valuable life experiences', with individual timetables and people filling their days with 'useful' and 'fulfilling' activities. In reality this was not possible for a hundred people every day, so some people sat and read magazines when they had nothing else to do. Over the years, this had become a group activity in itself.

This was a Tuesday morning, and so George was looking at magazines. Or at least he was pretending to whenever a member of staff came in.

They were in one of the smaller rooms, and the members of the magazine reading group were sitting around small tables. There was a table in the corner with a pile of magazines messily spilling over onto the floor. Everyone in the group had gone right through the whole pile to pick out their favourite, so that table was in a big mess now. As the group were on their own most of the time, they were playing at doing impressions of the staff – barely looking at the magazines at all. They were taking it in turns to do impressions to the whole group and the rule was you were not allowed to say who you were doing, everyone else had to guess.

The best person in the group was Tracy, George's girlfriend. She was so good, all she had to do was the face, she didn't need to say a word, and everyone could tell who she was. George loved watching Tracy do this. Partly it meant he could just gaze at her without it being obvious, and partly because she was really funny. George loved it when he laughed so much it made his nose make noises, and watching Tracy do her impression of the manager would make his nose snort like mad, which made him laugh even harder. She was great. He loved being with her, loved to be able to see her, or even just knowing she was there in the room with him was enough. Today George gazed and laughed and snorted and felt really happy . . . maybe Tuesdays were not so bad after all.

George loved Tracy so much that it hurt in his chest. He ached and sometimes cried in bed at night on his own. He wanted to be with her all the time. They did loads of things together, as much as possible. Tracy liked cooking too, so they went to College together and did some of the same classes. Tracy could read so she went to classes for that as well. George went to a computer class while Tracy did reading. He was not really interested in the computers or the stupid kid's games he had to play because he could not read. He only went because he got to be at College while Tracy was there. It gave them loads more time together.

George liked to kiss Tracy, a lot, especially at College where there were no staff to tell them to stop. They spent most of the time outside classes kissing, and it made George so happy he thought he would burst some days, because Tracy wanted to kiss him and be with him just as much as he wanted her. This surprised him a bit. He thought he was not very good looking really, and had been called all sorts of names, even in the street from people who had never seen him before; they would just look at his face and say rude things to him. George had always thought he must look really bad for this to happen to him. Tracy said she thought he was great, she told him that she really fancied him, and because he thought she was the most beautiful woman he had ever seen, he was not going to argue with her about him being too ugly for her. He never told her that he thought he would never be good enough for her, that she would meet someone else and suddenly realise he was not good enough. Until that happened he just wanted to be with her and kiss her all the time. And that was all he told her, that he loved her and thought she was beautiful. She always kissed him when he said this, so he told her very often.

*   *   *

Peter walked on through the cave, which was now practically level. He could see clearly as everything was lit with the same strange green luminescence that appeared to come from the rock itself. Nothing much seemed to happen for a while until he noticed something strange in the surface of the rock on his left. As he approached the rock seemed to shimmer slightly and he reached out to touch it. To his surprise his hand passed through the rock; clearly there was a hiding place in the wall here, and somehow some kind of hologram had been set up to look like the rock surface. Peter felt pleased with himself for not being fooled by this, and grabbed hold of whatever was in there and pulled it out. A shiver went down his spine when he saw that he had pulled out a gun. It was some kind of semi-automatic rifle, with some ammunition already in it. There was not much ammunition, and Peter reached into the rock again to check if there was any more in there. His hunch was right. He pulled out an ammo pack and put it straight in his belt.

The shiver had not been fear; Peter knew that whenever he found a weapon it meant he was going to get attacked soon. This was, of course, what he was here for, and the shiver had been one of excitement. While he was sorting out how to carry and use the weapon he heard a deep rumbling noise that reverberated in the rock. Peter could feel the noise in his feet as well as hear it. Great. Whatever it was, it was a distance away yet, which meant he had time to prepare. How though? How do you prepare for something you know nothing about?

At the moment there did not seem to be much he could do . . . he was in a cave – he could move forwards, stay still or go back the way he had come. He had to go forwards, and Peter ran on, towards that terrible noise. The sound grew louder as he got closer, he could feel the noise trembling in the rock all around him. As he ran forwards the rock above him got higher, and the walls to the side got further away. The cave got larger and larger until he came out into a cavern. The roof was so high he could barely see it, and the space was huge and echoed like a cathedral.

Over to his right Peter caught his first glimpse of what was making the noise. There were a few caves heading off from this central cavern, and a human shape had emerged from one of them at the same time as Peter had run out of his. It was massive, clearly three times the height of Peter, with a huge chest and clearly defined muscles in its legs. From this distance Peter could see it had rags for clothing, and he caught a glimpse of saliva dripping from razor-sharp teeth as it ran headlong, mouth wide open and roaring, into the opening. The heartbeat pause as it saw him gave Peter just enough time to raise his gun, only to see it disappear before his eyes.

Its skin had glowed with the same green light as the rocks and all around them. Then it was gone; as it saw him it had vanished into thin air. In his confusion Peter, his gun ready, shot straight at the place where he had seen it disappear. As the bullets landed the air seemed to shimmer slightly, like a heat wave, and the shimmering moved incredibly quickly over to the left, then stopped as suddenly as it had started. Peter wondered if it was able to make itself invisible, but only if it was still – what he could see was the air moving around it.

Thin air indeed.

That would mean that it was now standing very still exactly where the shimmering had stopped. The easiest way to test his theory was to shoot at that spot, which Peter did. He was right; the air shimmered for a short while moving straight towards him. He carried on shooting and the giant gave up trying to stay hidden and appeared before him. It had travelled with great speed and was merely feet away from him; Peter stepped backwards and shot straight at the creature's head. Blood poured from one of its eye sockets; it fell to its knees, groaned, gave off a blood-curdling shriek and exploded right in front of him. That was it. It had disappeared.

Peter breathed out with extreme relief and checked his ammo. It was low. If everything took that many bullets to kill he only had enough for one more fight. This was bad, and he scanned round the cavern searching the rock surface for more hidden holes where more ammo might be waiting for him. The surface of the rock was visibly different in three or four places. He ran over and reached into the closest one but what he pulled out was a first aid kit. This was bad. It was bad because it was not ammo, which he needed, but also it was bad because Peter knew that finding a first aid kit meant he was pretty certain to need one. Having used his last one fixing his wrists and shoulders on the way in, he needed another one anyway. He pocketed it and ran on to the next hole. Thankfully all the others had ammo in, and by the time he got to the last one he was fully loaded and ready for any number of invisible giants.

Peter froze for a moment, motionless and wondered briefly what was going on.

*   *   *

"What the hell do you think you're doing?!?"

Everyone in the room jumped out of their skin as Dave stormed in shouting.

"Tracy! Get down off that table. All of you go and sit back down. You can all wipe those smiles right off your faces. You're an absolute disgrace. You need staff in here to make sure you can look at a magazine? Can't you be trusted just to sit quietly for a morning? I'm busy in the other room and I cannot hear what people are saying to me because of the noise coming from this room! Honestly! What's the matter with you today? This is ridiculous. Do I need to find someone to sit in with you and watch you?"

No one said anything.

"Do I? Tracy, you were on the table doing God only knows what, do you need a member of staff in here to make sure the table does not get trodden all over again? Do I?"

"No," Tracy said. She said it really clearly, staring him down while she did it.

"Yes, well, I should hope not too. I'm going to go back to my class now, and if I hear one more squeak out of any of you for the rest of the morning I'll just have to bring my whole class in here with you. Do you understand?"

A couple of them nodded. They all had their heads down, staring at the magazines in front of them, waiting for him to just go away with a final,

"Right then."

They looked up and grinned at each other. Barry, who was supposed to have been keeping a look out for staff coming in, whispered across to them.

"I'm really, really sorry, I been laughing at Tracy with all you."

He had come away from the door and had been caught up in the fun, clapping and whistling with everyone else. Of course they knew it had got out of hand, but Tracy had just got into doing Mrs Jackson as a stripper off the telly, which was hysterical. They all forgave Barry, none of them had noticed Dave either.

Tracy had got carried away with being a stripper. She'd seen something on the TV with women dancing on a stage with the men all around the edges of the stage. This was what she had tried to recreate. She had needed to be above everyone so she could do it like they had on the TV, and wiggle her bum down at their faces. Of course she had only shown her bum to George, none of the other men, she had really liked teasing him like that. He was so obviously embarrassed and excited at the same time. She liked that she could make him feel like that.

*   *   *

Susan loved her computer. It was new, powerful and came with loads of add-ons. It was the best combined birthday and Christmas present she had ever had. It had been worth the wait until Christmas too, because she got the latest, fastest new Pentium ∞ system, which had not been out for her birthday.

The computer had come with a game she had just started. Reading the box it looked like a standard quest game, and the layout looked a lot like the ancient and now defunct *Tomb Raider*, except the character was male. She had, typically for her, not read through the instructions . . . or viewed any of the back-story . . . she had just started playing. She knew she had done pretty well to get through as far as she had without getting killed, so having killed the first of the enemies she had found, she had saved the game and sat back to view other menu items to find the story which started it all off. This, she hoped, would give her some idea what she was supposed to do in these caves, where to head for, what to kill, what to collect and so on.

She sat back, expecting it to be the usual high graphic storyboard type of intro. She was given two choices though, 'Introduction' or 'Interactive'. She clicked on 'Interactive'; she could always come back to the 'Introduction' later if she still wanted to. The first thing she was asked for was her name, which she typed in, then her age and a description, height, hair colour, age. She was a little unnerved about all this, and not experienced enough to know that she could make stuff up. When prompted to ask if she wanted to start a gaming journal she was stumped. Reaching for the box she finally got out the instruction sheets and lay on the bed to read them.

It turned out this was 'a new generation of gaming experience' and had been 'conceived to take full advantage of the maximum capabilities of the new Pentium ∞ processor'. The 'Fully Interactive Joystick' supplied still lay in the box. Susan had never used one before; she had always played games using the keyboard controls on her Dad's old work computer.

She skipped through the descriptions of the 'retro graphics style' as she had already seen the game. She wanted to know what made this one so different from all the others; her interest was in the term 'fully interactive'. Finally she got to the interesting part. She had to read it through twice to make sure she had fully understood what it was saying. It turned out the character in the game was some kind of intelligent program. This meant it could learn from its environment, and from input from the player. The gaming journal she had been asked to set up was a key part of his learning. The other part was the new joystick. It had sensors in the grip handle which monitored pulse rate and sweat content of the player, which informed the emotional state of the gaming character. Susan decided this sounded really cool, went back to the computer and clicked on 'yes' to set up her gaming journal.

The first question she was asked made no sense to her at all.

"How old were you when you were captured?"

At this point she realised she would have to watch the Introduction. She came out of that menu and returned to the beginning to get the Introduction.

This time she could just sit back and watch. The story was told on the computer exactly like a piece of film. A voice-over told the story, while the action described was played out in front of her. The graphics were much better quality than the actual game.

"Once upon a time there was an old King who had two children, a son and a daughter. The son was the elder and had been raised since birth to some day be King. He had always been given the best

of everything: food, clothes, jewels and education. He had never wanted for anything and he had grown up spoilt and arrogant. Many of the courtiers could see that there was going to be trouble when his turn came to rule the land. The old King could see this in his headstrong son, and had not abdicated his throne, in the hope that the young man would somehow gain wisdom and insight before he became King.

The daughter was kind, gentle and humble, raised since birth to serve her older brother. She was well read and had never lacked for anything. She had watched and listened and learned about the world and the way of people. She was kind to everyone, and never questioned her brother in any way.

As time went on the son grew jealous of his younger sister. He saw the way she was treated by the courtiers about the palace, and he watched his father, the King, offering her smiles and fond embraces he never offered to his heir. With time this so enraged the young man he decided his sister must be forced to leave the palace. With her gone he believed his father would love him as he so clearly loved her.

The son plotted with his manservant to have her taken and abandoned in a cavern he had heard of, hidden deep in a labyrinth of caves away in the mountains to the East. She was to be given enough food to survive until the death of the King, at which point she would be brought home to attend the public funeral and then to serve him, her brother, the new King.

The King was informed that his daughter had decided to leave while he was still healthy and fit, to see more of the world, the better to help her brother when he reigned over the kingdom.

Meanwhile the manservant secretly took the King's daughter away at night, and travelled with her to the East. There he found the labyrinth of caves deep inside a mountain. Locking her in a cavern, he left her with enough food and water to last many years. She had no light and no one knew she was there.

Now, the young heir to the throne did not know that his sister had a secret love, Oemor, who adored her more than the sun and the moon. They had sworn to marry some day when Oemor had made his fortune; until then their love was known only to themselves. On hearing of her *disappearance Oemor knew that his love would never leave in such a manner without telling him, and so he knew that the story that had been told by the prince was untrue.*

Being good friends with the manservant, Oemor took the man out for food and wine and then plied him with whisky before asking questions about the disappearance of the young woman. The manservant, feeling warm and affectionate to the generous Oemor, his good and trusted friend, told everything. It did not take long for Oemor to get a full description of how to find the caves to the East of the land, and how it would be possible to rescue his beloved before the King died.

Oemor set off the next day towards the East and soon found the mountain range the servant had described so well. However, he was rushing so hard as he looked for the entrance that he accidentally fell into a deep shaft leading to a different part of the caves."

This is where the introduction stopped, and clearly where the game Susan had played yesterday had started. The computer returned to the Interactive screen, and Susan embarked on answering the questions for setting up her gaming journal.

She thought it was a pretty lame story, but this stuff about monitoring her and integrating what was going on with her pulse rate into the game was cool. It was also fairly cool to play a part in the game; Oemor (what a terrible name for a hero, she thought) was coming to rescue *her!* It was romantic, and it was a game she already knew she was good at. Susan was confident that this was going to be fun.

Chapter 2

Tracy thought George was the best thing that had ever happened to her. He was gentle, kind and loving to her, he was handsome, and good with his hands. She liked to watch him cook. She would imagine the way he handled the food was the way he would touch her when they made love. He clearly loved the food and took pride in what he did. He was a good cook too; it was the only thing he could do better than her. She could never be bothered to wait and do things right, she always wanted to just get on and eat. George could follow a recipe exactly, and once he had learned it, he did it perfectly every time.

As their relationship had gone on Tracy had started to wonder whether they actually would make love. For all she could watch him, and imagine how good it might be, there never seemed to be a place or a time where they could go and be together in that way. She also had started to wonder lately whether George would know the recipe if they ever got there. She could see that once he knew what to do he would do it perfectly every time, but she was not sure he would know exactly what to do. Come to think of it, she was not sure she knew exactly what to do either, but she knew she wanted more than kissing in the corridors.

Tracy could read very well, and she was so proud of this that she read everything she could get hold of. Most of the time this was magazines and the books Mum got out of the library and the drivel she had to wade through at College. She hated that College class, she wanted Mills and Boon not Janet and John, and she only went because it was another chance to be with George. College was easier than the day centre, and he was more relaxed and talked more away from there. Also they got to kiss loads, which she loved. It was worth sitting through the reading class just to get that time with him.

Apart from the College books everything Tracy read was from

magazines and cheap books and so everything she read was about men and sex and relationships. She had learned that this was what life was all about, and this was what Tracy wanted more than anything else; to have a boyfriend, to have sex with him and to have a baby. That was why when George had asked her to be his girl she felt like she was going to burst with happiness and pride.

One down, two to go.

Tracy thought from kissing in the corridors that George wanted more with her. Not that he ever talked about it, but she could feel that his body got hard and pressed against her, so she knew he really wanted her. She loved this feeling, and pressed herself against him so she could feel him touching her through their clothes. She wanted them to be able to take their clothes off and lie down; she wanted to feel his body. She also wanted to look at him naked and see what he looked like, but she thought this might be a bit embarrassing for him, she was just really curious about his body. Tracy realised that as George did not read at all he might not know that they could take their clothes off and do more with their bodies. He never talked about wanting to do anything but kiss, and Tracy was starting to get impatient.

One of the things Tracy liked about George was that he was also Downs. This was what she was called, 'A Downs', and she knew that he was one too. Tracy had figured that they looked different to other people, particularly around the eyes, and they had lovely short, wide bodies, which she liked. Having short bodies meant everyone looked down at them, and treated them as though they were below them. Tracy had guessed that this was why she was called 'Downs'. George was so lovely because he never treated her like that at all. They were almost exactly the same height, and he treated her with a respect and deference that made her feel completely special and better than anyone. He also had a way about him that made him special. Tracy thought it was because he could not read, and had a good Mum and Dad who loved him. He did not seem to know what the world was like, he did not know that people could be cruel or hurt him or be nasty at all. George lived as though everyone was as gentle and kind as he was. Tracy noticed that in general this meant people were really gentle and kind to him. She could see that people did not treat him like a man. No one thought of George as a man but her. And she thought of him as *her* man.

Tracy also knew they could not have sex without people being upset with them, and she did not know how George would feel about that. Downs like them did not do that . . . she knew that. That made her want it more, just to show them. She had got herself a man, and she wanted to have a proper family with him, Downs or no Downs. Tracy wanted to be an 'Ups', and she was going to make it happen.

*   *   *

George was in his room. He had masturbated quietly and was lying on his bed daydreaming about Tracy. She always made him feel like that, like rubbing himself down there, it felt so good all over his body. What he really wanted was for Tracy to be there when it happened, maybe even touch him, but he worried she would be revolted by him doing something rude like that. George was afraid he would probably lose her if he suggested anything like that to her.

He also thought it would feel amazing if she did.

His mind had wandered onto other things. George's room was in the attic and he had a window above his head, which meant he could look up at the sky while lying in bed. He really liked this window. Today there was a beautiful bright blue sky with fluffy white clouds floating across the framed view. He played a bit at guessing what the clouds were. Some looked like animals, some like vehicles. He liked it best when he could look at one cloud and watch it change from one thing into another as it floated past the window. As he lay there watching the clouds George drifted off to sleep, warm, comfortable and feeling happy about Tracy and how much he loved her.

George understood writing like a fish understands a tree. It cast a shadow over areas of his life, he knew it was there, and he could do nothing about it. Today George dreamt he could read. He dreamt about this quite often and had done so since he was a child at school, when he first learned that there was something most people did that he could not.

Today his dream was in a bright sunlit field. He and Tracy were lying holding hands, she was leaning over him and staring at him, talking and laughing. She had a book, and was showing him a page of it, pointing to a particular passage. He sat up slightly on one elbow, grinned at her and read the part her finger was pointing to. George dreamt that the words had meaning; through just his eyes looking at the paper, he understood something new and funny. He laughed at what he had read, leaned forward and kissed Tracy, taking her cheek in his hand and she said "dinner time" before he lay back down again. George woke up and knew that his mother had called for him to go down for dinner. Waking slightly confused in this way he waited a moment to try and remember what it was in his dream that he had read, but all he could remember was what had happened, and the feeling of the sun and the wind in the field.

*   *   *

Susan jumped as she heard the front door slam shut and George running straight upstairs to his room, banging the door behind him. What day was it? Must be a College day, she thought. He'd been snogging with that girlfriend of his and had to have a wank as soon as he got in. Susan wished they could sort it out for George to actually have sex with her and get it over with, but she knew Mum and Dad would never let that happen.

She was busy with the computer game. Having read through all the instructions she could find and watched the full introduction story she had started to fill in all the questions. She figured if she was going to do this thing at all she might as well do it right.

Susan was about halfway through setting up her journal options when she spotted an extra scan picture option. She knew that Dad's new fax machine also had a scanner in it, and he had spent some time carefully getting old family photos onto his office PC. She knew that there was a photo of her, a school one, on her computer. Dad had said that he had set it up with one there in case she ever needed it for school.

It did not take her long to set the journal up with that photo.

She was just about coming to the end of the gaming journal questions when she heard Mum calling for dinner. Her mind was absorbed completely in what she had been doing. The questions had been personal and difficult to answer. Susan had answered all of them as openly and honestly as she could. She had never had a diary before, and was not used to writing about her thoughts and feelings. The computer seemed the best place for her to be frank about her inner feelings. It was inanimate, uncaring and unresponsive. Like a teddy bear, but without the cuddly face. She liked that.

Sighing to herself with annoyance at the interruption, she came out of her room and practically collided with George. He looked dazed like he had just woken up, and he went to the bathroom on his way down.

Good.

This way we don't have to walk into the kitchen together, so I won't be mean to him straight away. Poor guy did not deserve that.

She wanted to eat and run back upstairs as quickly as possible, needing to get straight back into the game.

The new joystick was unwrapped, plugged in and waiting for her.

*   *   *

Oemor was confused and disorientated.

He could remember being Peter, he knew how to use a gun and was strong and confident. He remembered how he had fought one of the 'Nephillim'. Strange that he knew a name for the giants now.

Now he was Oemor. He was hopelessly in love with Susan, who was trapped in a cavern, and determined to save her no matter what the cost. He was going to have to fight more. Oemor knew everything Peter had known, felt everything Peter had felt. Peter knew there would be more fighting because he had found more bullets for the gun and a first aid kit. Oemor knew it because he could hear the same noise rumbling through the rock, sounding as though it was heading his way. This time there would be no running towards them. For one thing he was still in the huge cavern with four or five caves leading off from it, he had no idea which tunnel they were coming down. The other reason he could not run headlong towards his foe was that Oemor was experiencing something Peter had never felt; he was frightened. As the noise had vibrated through his feet from the rock, and echoed round the cavern, he had felt a knot grow in his stomach, a tightening of his fingers on the gun, and an urge to run in the opposite direction from the noise. Thankfully for Oemor, in that moment of first feeling, he still had no idea where they were coming from. Knowing he could just as easily be running straight at them kept his feet planted firmly on the ground, immovable.

There was something else that kept him there – a note of reason. Peter had realised, and so now Oemor also knew, that he was safer out here. It was his only chance to see where the Nephillim were. If he went into one of the smaller caves, all they would have to do is stand perfectly still until he was practically underneath them. He shuddered at the thought of how they could make themselves invisible and clutched the gun closer, somehow safer.

There, to the left.

Oemor managed to spin round and fire the gun simultaneously, relieved to find he still had all of Peter's skills with the weapon. As he did so he caught sight of another emerging from a cave straight ahead of him, closely followed by another. He spun to his right and fired, spun straight round to his left and fired – a wide spread of bullets, only some of which actually hit his enemy, the others ricocheted off the rock surface behind them. The level of noise, and the bullets that hit home made it impossible for the three Nephillim to keep still, so Oemor could see them all the time. Soon he had killed them all without wasting too many bullets. The last one had got very close, and by the time it was all over he had a large gash in his arm. He had been terrified, he could feel his heart rate in a completely different way. Rather than just hearing it, he could actually feel it beating inside his chest. He was shaking and sweating and felt exhausted. He knew he had to rest, get his heart rate down, and try and think about what had happened to him and to Peter.

Peter had known what his heart rate was, but just as passive knowledge, like reading a chart. This was completely different. To be able to feel it shaking in his throat was a bit scary in itself. He sat down, or at least, he collapsed to the ground and leant on the wall behind him. As he used his first aid kit on the wound in his arm his heart sank as he felt the rock tremble against his back; more were on their way. He got to his feet, picked up the gun, and leaped in shock as he noticed he was practically out of bullets. It did not seem possible . . . he had had so many. What he had left was less than it had taken him to kill just one. Chances were that there was more than one on their way again this time. This meant he needed to go into one of the smaller caves, just to pick up more ammo. Realistically he knew he was also likely to need more first aid.

Oemor knew that with so little ammo, he had more chance of a direct hit with every bullet if he was in a confined space than out here in the open. He also knew that the best way to do this was to wait until they emerged, so he could see which caves they came out from, and then run as fast as he could down a different cave. Oemor knew that he had to find Susan as soon as possible. His heart ached to be with her again. He knew which direction he had entered the cavern, the one now over to his left. So he knew which direction he needed to go to carry on . . . the cave to his right. He guessed that this would take him further into the centre of the caves, which was where he needed to go.

As he was working this out a Nephillim emerged roaring from the very cave he wanted to go down. Oemor ran headlong into the closest cave regardless of the direction. It was amazing how fast they could move, how sharp their teeth were, how frightened he felt. He ran so hard he was afraid his legs would not move fast enough to keep him from falling forwards. The entire cave shook with a roar from the Nephillim, indicating to Oemor that it was in the same tunnel as him now. This was an overwhelming sensation of noise and tremor that knocked him off his feet. Peter's fighting instincts took over and enabled him to roll straight round as he fell, so he landed facing the Nephillim with his gun into its face, and fired. The Nephillim screamed, exploded and vanished just as quickly.

Breathing a shaky sigh of relief Oemor realised the rock face next to his head was shimmering; he reached in and grabbed the ammo he so desperately needed. Even in this panic-stricken state he still had the presence of mind to try again in the same hole. This time he pulled out a first aid kit. Damn, he thought. Oemor already knew what that meant, and sure enough, he heard a second Nephillim enter his cave. Still on his back, with the gun pointing upwards, he decided to stay where he was. Running was pointless as they were so fast and he would be facing the wrong way when it reached him. This way he could fire at the first shimmer in the air. Even if the thing was invisible he would still get it. He waited. All he could hear was his own pulse.

Everything had gone quiet; Oemor knew it was too quiet, that something was not right. He did not realise until it was much, much too late what it was that had gone wrong. Oemor did not realise until he was dying that another Nephillim had been coming down the cave behind him. It was waiting in the silence. Oemor did not realise it was there until he saw flesh-riddled teeth above his forehead, felt teeth in the base of his neck, and he screamed the one name that had any meaning,

"SUSAN!!"

Susan jumped out of her chair.
"Wow!"
She was impressed. This whole game was amazing. The contact with the joystick had given the game a whole new depth. The audible breathing of the guy . . . what was his stupid name . . . had matched her own breath throughout. She could feel her own pulse rate through it, and she had felt really frightened. She checked her armpits as she sat back down. Yes, she really had been sweating with fear. She had never done that with just a dumb game before. She checked the logo on the joystick, and realised it was not the maker's logo, but the name of the game itself, *Nephillim Caves*. This stick had been designed and produced purely for this one game. All the technology for tracking her pulse and bodily reactions, that was brand new just for this. She wondered if this was going to be how all gaming felt in the future.

Instead of going back to a screen where she could return to the last saved game, the computer was showing her a journal entry. She remembered now, she had said she wanted to update her journal every death. At the time this option for updates had just sounded a bit Goth and cool. Now she realised two things; that she wanted to update it more often than that . . . if she got really good at this hopefully there would not be that many more deaths, and secondly that she really did want to write about how she was feeling. After filling in all those questions, she now wanted to share more.

There was something about the way he had called out her name . . . *her name* . . . when he died. Such passion in his voice had shocked, but also moved her. To hear anyone say her name with such feeling. It was so different to the way she usually heard her voice shouted – her Mum in anger – this was different. This was a new emotion she had never heard before. Even if he was just a computer game Susan felt herself blushing at the screen as it faded back to the menu.

It was while she was writing the journal that Susan heard the knock on her door. It was a gentle knock, and she knew she could ignore it if she wanted, but not this time, she wanted so much to tell someone about this, and George was the only person she felt she could. She called for him to come in without stopping typing, she did not want to lose her thought, and George would not know what it said anyway, so she might as well carry on.

"Hi, Sue," said George. It was a sign of how much she liked him that she let him call her Sue. No one else could be that familiar with her at the moment, and her Mum did not like it to be abbreviated.

"We gave you that name because it sounded nice as it is, so please use it that way. We wanted you to sound like you had a nice name."

Susan felt it was also a terrible testament that her parents were complete losers that they had named her after a film star without realising, they just thought it sounded nice. What wasters!

"Hi, George, whatsup?"

"Well . . . erm, Sue, I was wondering what was going on?"

"What do you mean?" She glanced round and motioned with her head for him to sit on the bed.

"All the noise, Sue, you know? What's all the noise? I can hear in my room, shouts and guns, and someone yelled your name. I got scared, I didn't know what was going on, and so I came down to ask you, Sue, what's happening?"

George had been staring at the computer while he had been talking. He was distracted by how her computer looked compared

25

with the ones he used at College. This one the screen was big and flat with black edges. It looked like it had proper pictures in it, not like the kids games he played at College. He could see that she was writing though, so he guessed you would have to know how to read to know how to work it.

"Oh God, sorry, George, I forgot I had the sound up so high, I wasn't wearing headphones. Shit, did Mum and Dad hear it too? I'm surprised they're not bawling me out right now."

"No, they went out after dinner. They said the pub, and asked if I'd be all right. I was going to go to bed. I'm really tired."

"Yeh, I bet you are." She threw him a sly glance, but he was not looking. George was still staring at the computer. "So, listen, I'll put my headphones on OK? Then you can get some sleep. I'm sorry, I forgot."

"It's OK."

He waited a moment.

"Sue?"

"Yeh?"

"What's going on?"

"What do you mean?" Susan had turned back to face the screen, thinking he would go.

"All the noise, Sue, what is all the noise, you know?"

"Oh. Right. It's this new game that came with the computer."

"That's a computer game? Firing and guns and screaming your name . . . is a game? Wow. Really? That's not like the games at College!"

"No! I bet it's not. What do you do at College?"

"It's just kids stuff." He hung his head as he said this. He was her older brother, and he did not like it that as she was growing up he could see her doing things he had never done. She was so much younger than him, nearly 12 years. How come she was playing a proper game on a proper computer in her own bedroom, while he had to go to College and play *Find The Mouse*?

Susan turned round and looked at him. His head was hanging down and his face was flushed. She had known for ages that she could do things George could not, like reading and maths, but lately she noticed she was doing things he had never done, and getting presents he had never got. She had started to hate it as much as he clearly did. She hated that Mum and Dad, and everyone else, made him so different, when he was not really all that different, once you got to know him. Although in the past she had always thought of this in terms of how much she hated Mum and Dad and how horrible they were. Right now looking at him sitting on her bed, she felt sorry for him and how he must feel. She wanted to offer him something.

"Hey, George, you wanna see the game? It's amazing." She was not sure it would help really, but it might be fun to show him.

"Let me finish writing this and I'll show you how it works."

George's face was transformed, although she did not see it. He had hoped she would let him see her new computer sometime. He knew she had really liked it at Christmas because she had not said anything bad about it at all. He had not seen much of her since, and this was the first time Mum and Dad had gone out while both Susan and he were both in and up for ages. He grinned and nodded and waited, gazing at the screen, mesmerised by the light and the growing lines of words appearing on it.

"Right then, I'll just save this and we'll have a look at it together. I just got killed, which is what the screaming was about, so I'll have to go to the last time I saved it. That'll give you a good feel for the graphics 'cos it's in this huge cavern."

Oemor was confused and disorientated. He could remember being Peter, then he could remember being himself here in exactly the same place, and killing more Nephillim, then running down a tunnel, killing another one and having his head bitten off.

Here he was though, alive, with loads of ammo, exactly where he had been, and he heard the rumbling in the rock and calling of the three Nephillim as they approached him. This time he knew which caves they were coming out of, and he knew he had killed them last time, so he felt less frightened. Oemor stepped toward the cave entrance he knew two of them were going to come out of. He fired straight at them, accurate and smooth, he felt in control and confident. The creatures exploded with their ear-splitting shriek one after the other; he easily spun round to the one that had come from the left after killing the first two and got it before it reached him.

Excellent! He was, for the moment, safe, with loads more ammo and a first aid kit unused this time. He knew again that they were coming, and thought he could remember where from. He certainly knew which cave he had gone down and died. This time the decision was more complicated. Should he go down the same cave, but shoot in front of him as well as behind? Knowing what was there could be a big advantage, or should he just try a different cave? He thought he would go to the same cave and try facing the enemy he knew.

To his terror found that he could not move. Not just his feet, but also his arms and head as well. It was completely quiet, nothing was happening, and he could not move, he was just standing there.

"I'll pause it there, while he's safe," Susan said as she turned to see George's face, wide eyed and staring. She could tell he was hooked. She explained how the joystick felt her own heartbeat, and how the game echoed her breathing rate. She told him the story from the introduction, about Oemor and the King's daughter and that he was shooting giants in the caves because he was on his way to rescue her. This was a bit complicated, and she told him that she was playing a part in the game – the Princess that Oemor was coming to rescue was her. She said how she had entered details about herself, and as she explained it, she realised that this was how he had called out her name. His character was in love with her.

George listened, completely absorbed. He said it sounded like a fairy tale. Then he started asking about whether guns had been around in fairy-tale times. This annoyed Susan a bit. Not so much that he clearly had never played games like this because anyone who had would know they all use guns, but more because she had not thought of it herself. Clearly though, no one could fight these giants with just a sword, which is what she said to him.

She told him about Oemor having his head bitten off and enjoyed the look of revulsion on his face. They had a long, involved chat about what 'sentient' meant. The information had said that Oemor was a new generation of learning, sentient programs. To try and explain it more Susan got out the instructions and information. She had read all of this herself, so she just skimmed through for George what she knew and how she understood it.

George was fascinated, and sat on her bed, enraptured by everything she told him. Susan was talking really quickly; she always did when she was excited. George knew that the only thing to do was just sit and let the words wash over him, and then think about them later. George had learned to do this as a way of understanding what people were saying when they did not talk slowly for him. He would lie in bed at the end of the day and think over what people said. He could remember really well, and at night he could slow it all down and hear it through again. While they were talking all he could do was sit and let the words drift over him.

This meant that any questions he might have would have to wait. He would have to ask Susan later, and he knew she might not talk with him like this about it again. He just sat and listened as well as he could, and made sure he asked everything he could think of here and now while he had the chance.

*   *   *

CP4You were the largest manufacturers of cheap computers in the western world. In the early years of business growth they realised that the best way to get computer shoppers to buy their computer instead of a rival's was to give away free games. First of all they bought these in, but this had a detrimental effect on the cash flow forecast and year-end projections that the stockholders were unhappy about. After doing some calculations, and successfully applying for research grant funding, they set up their own development unit to design their own games. As with everything else *CP4You* did, the games development unit was the best in the business; they produced high quality very quickly.

The research grant was awarded for research into artificial intelligence, and had been gained through the Defence Experimentation and Improvement section of the Government's Military Grant Programme. The people they employed to work on developing the new games were from a range of backgrounds.

Some were programmers, some were hackers, and a few were from military intelligence – they came with the grant. The company invested heavily in team building and sharing expertise, and it was not too long before *CP4You* had the best team at the forefront of Sentient Technology development. The military would not claim ownership until the whole computer programme was perfected, and in the meantime *CP4You* were the only gaming manufacturers with intelligent gaming characters. The only way to get hold of one of their games was to buy a *CP4You* computer, and everyone wanted to try out the new characters who learned from their experiences through *intuition* rather than pre-programmed logic. It was a market winner.

All successful businesses cut corners wherever savings can be made, which means wherever they cannot be detected by the customer. *CP4You* were no exception.

They had launched the new 'learning, fighting soldiers' characters in a platform game called *Megadeath* with the new Pentium 4 launch. The game involved 12 soldiers with the first basic Sentient Technology program. Each of the twelve then had personality traits individually built on top of the original program. The personality traits were partly to individualise the soldiers, and partly to ensure they functioned as a complete fighting unit, with pack instincts and an established pecking order. Matthew and Mark were the rival leaders, and the others were followers with specific skills.

By the time *Megadeath 7* came out it was the last of the Pentium 4 upgrades and they had already started developing a whole new game and structure for the next processor launch. Once they had the basic program for intuitive learning, they kept it as the foundations for a solo gaming character. All the individualised personality traits, which were fiddly and expensive to write raw code for, were launched during the introduction sequences the first time the game was played. It was a cheap way of cutting down on programming time. Simple variations at the launch of identical programs would result in variations in behaviour, increasing during play as experiences and individual game-play varied. Essentially everyone who played would end up playing a different game, because the data they entered in the gaming journal about themselves would be unique. This information was then written in to the program during the launch program. This was ultimately the great selling value of intuitive learning programs that they aimed to flood the market with.

The researchers at *CP4You* kept accurate figures on buying trends, population's tendencies and gender preferences. They knew that the *Megadeath* series had attracted almost exclusively men. They were satisfied that they were selling to black, white, poor, rich, young and old, but all men. This had left a gap in the market, which they knew was a growing independent home Personal Computer purchasing market – women.

For the new game designed to launch the new processor, they needed to develop a game that would capture that market, and keep all the existing male customers. This was a real challenge. In order to cut costs they took the original basic 'intelligence' program from the *Megadeath* series. To make it a workable game as a solo player adventure, they used the Scout Soldier, Peter, who had individual personality programming to work independently from the others. In order to use the 'Peter' program as the basic building blocks for the new character, they launched the *Megadeath* soldier (simply by starting the game through the introduction screens) saved the game and cut his raw code from the existing source. This way they had raw code for an independent soldier with self-preservation and fighting skills as the new basic program, before the new introduction, and the personality traits were built in by the journal entries of each customer.

The storyboard people created a fairy-tale romance story to hang a basic platform game on. Research had shown that women wanted to play 'shoot-em-up' style games, but did not want to see so much of the violence. They wanted to kill enemies and use guns, but wanted to do it for the right reasons. The storyboard developers, who were all men, thought that love was the only reason good enough for this kind of heroism, so the programmers, who were also all men, wrote a program for love. This would be the new program launched through the introduction schemes. It was complex code, and would rely heavily on the player's gaming strategy as to how the love sub-routines would respond. The gaming programmers then added some extra areas of gaming play which would only be reached if players did different things. This was possible with intuitive learning, and meant that each player would end up with a radically different game, depending on how they interacted with their character.

They also thought it would be good to write some basic fear responses in as well, to get a feel of hero, not soldier.

The new gaming interface, (through the joystick's pulse-rate monitor and 'gaming journal recognition and interpretation technology') would give the new program information about how the gamer was feeling, but it would be better if that was mutual. The joystick interface was the most exciting part of the new game development. To program in a way of incorporating the gamer's feelings with the sentient program was the biggest challenge they had faced since they first developed the learning program. They knew it was going to be good. What they did not know was that it was going to be two way.

As the basic 'intelligent' program, Peter, was released with the game unplayed, it was only through the introductory pages launching the personality traits to incorporate the gamer's specific details, that the new character, Oemor, could be born. He would be 'born' slightly differently depending on how the gaming journal questions were answered. If the gamer was male or female, the game was different. This was how they intended to keep the male market and catch a new female market at the same time.

If the player was female, the intention was for the new character, Oemor, to start the game 'in love with' the gamer herself. The 'relationship development' sub-programs would be launched by the gaming journal inputs. A relationship would develop between the character and the gamer as the game was played.

All of this was brand new.

The programmers worked hard and they worked well. The whole development team was, by now, well established. The guys who designed the pulse monitors for the joysticks were drinking buddies with the love development programmers. The storyboard writers played poker every Friday with the market trend diagnosis and interpretation team. They developed, they programmed, they created and they successfully sold.

Some of the programmers included complex, experimental sub-routines which they knew would probably never be triggered. It turned out that most of the programmers had their own experimental coding they had been working on. By the time the game was released it was clear to them that the game would never play the same way twice, they had included so many variable options.

In all this work, no one considered the possibility that a seventeen-year-old girl on Christmas Day afternoon would be so excited and impatient that she would start the gaming character 'cold', as Peter. Only later, having played the game, would she read her instructions and go through the introduction to launch Oemor, in love, frightened, and with an unplanned but clear memory of actually being Peter.

But then, no one working at *CP4You* had ever met Susan.

Chapter 3

George was sitting in his jigsaw group a few days after Susan had shown him the new computer game. He was slouched over the table with his chin resting heavily on his fist, gazing unfocused at the jigsaw pieces in front of him. He was thinking about Susan's game, and wondering what it felt like to actually play it. How the joystick would feel, what a pulse rate was, and how close you had to get to be able to see Oemor's face.

Tracy came in with a piece of paper clutched in her hand, grinning at him. She spread the sheet out on the table in front of him so he could see it covered in words and some pictures.

"What does it say?" George asked. Then as an afterthought he realised,

"You're not supposed to be in here."

"Yeh I know," she waved dismissively "but look at this George, one of us could do this."

"What does it say?"

"*Are you unhappy or bored with your life? Would you like to be living the way you want? We can help you make changes in your life, get more of what you really want; less of what you do not want. We would like to lend you a hand, so give us a ring*, then there's the name Tim Sherman and a number to ring. George, we could do this and ask them to help us get on!"

"What do you mean? I'm not unhappy, I'm happy. Ask anyone, they'll tell you, Tracy, George is always happy."

"But George," she leaned forward, over the table and took his hand. She stared at him intently. She was about to say something really important and George suddenly felt his stomach turn over. Her voice was low, her gaze intent on his face.

"Don't you want us to get on? To move out from Mum's house and have our own house? And our own family? Don't you ever think about that, George? Don't you want that for us? You want to stay living at home all your life? 'Cos I certainly don't, George, no way. Don't you want to live with me?"

George had done what he always did when people spoke quickly, he had let the words wash over him so he could hear them in his head slower later and think about it. He had tried to let Tracy's words wash over him but instead they had washed right through him. He was surprised that she felt like that about him, and surprised that he had never thought that about her. He was profoundly, deeply moved. His stomach again rolled heavily down to his crotch, his head spun, he hoped he would not throw up on her and he held onto the desk and her hand to stay stable.

He gazed at her searchingly, she was not joking with him, and he realised that her face was crumpling, he was not saying anything and she must be thinking he was going to say no. He knew he had to say something, anything, to rescue her from his silence. He could not move, let alone pour out in words the wave of pure love and emotion that was crashing all over him. All he could do was tighten his grip on her hand and squeeze out the only tiny word he was capable of saying,

"Yes."

"Yes?"

"Yes, yes, I want that."

He felt it as he said it, more than anything else, of course, he wanted to live with her! It made sense, she was the one true love of his life.

Tears came out of their eyes at the same time, right there in front of each other, his were surfeit of emotion, and hers were relief. They held each other tight, falling together, crumpling the sheet of paper between them and knocking jigsaw pieces onto the floor. They stayed in this tight hug for a long time, her on her knees at his feet, him leaning down to clutch her around the waist.

When George thought about it afterwards he could not quite remember how it had all started, he could only remember that Tracy wanted him, in a way he had not dared to imagine, she really did want him like he wanted her.

They were going to live together.

He was not sure who to talk to about it, or how to make it happen.

He went to the most obvious person first, Susan, to ask her about what to say to Mum and Dad, which made her the first person he told.

She was in her room, headphones on and joystick in hand, sweating slightly and breathing heavily into the computer screen. George had learnt quickly that there was no way to get her attention while she had headphones on without making her jump. Although he had found this funny she had been really angry and had yelled at him. He backed quietly out of the room, and waited for Mum to call them down to dinner. He sat at the bottom of the small staircase which led to his bedroom, where he could be just out of sight when she came out. It was dark and a little bit chilly on the wooden steps. He sat hunched over, hugging his knees, as though he were hiding in a cupboard, and waited.

When Susan came out of her room, he followed her to the top of the stairs going down, and as she turned she still jumped slightly to see him right behind her.

"Hi, Sue, have you got time later . . . I mean, you know . . . to talk? I need to talk."

She grinned at him.

"Yeh, no problem, come knock on my door later eh?"

She turned away and completely ignored him after that.

She did this a lot, being nice sometimes and then horrible to him others. He had figured out that she was only nice to him when they were on their own, so he tried to talk to her properly then. So far it was working, and George was happy for them to ignore each other and just watch the TV while they ate. It was the typical frosty silence of a Sarandon household meal.

Sometimes George hated it when it was so quiet, he knew it meant his Mum and Dad had been arguing again, and he always felt worse when they sat so quietly. The silence seemed to be loud in the room and it put George off his food. Today, however, George did not mind the silence. He started to daydream about living with Tracy. George thought that there would never be silence like this in a house that he and Tracy lived in. If it was quiet that would be nice, but there would not be silence like this, not because they had been shouting at each other, like Mum and Dad or Mum and Susan did all the time.

Eating a meal in a house with Tracy! This made George smile to himself.

Tracy and he would sit at a table, not in front of the TV, and they would talk about their day. George would have cooked for her. He had so often daydreamed about cooking food for Tracy, it was good to be able to imagine her eating with him as well. He liked to cook vegetables because he liked all the preparation. Peeling and chopping, getting the timing right so everything was ready at the same time. George loved it most when he had enough time to chop everything up on clean wooden chopping boards first, to see it all laid out in bright, fresh colours, before he heated any water or poured any oil. When he lived with Tracy, George thought, he would always have time to chop everything first. He breathed a long sigh of pure happiness over his beans.

"You know Tracy?"
"She's your girlfriend at the centre?"
"Yeh, but . . . you know . . . I see her at College too."
"OK. What about her?"
"She asked me, she said she wants to move in with me. You know? For us to get a house, together, the two of us, for us to be together, you know? She wants us to have a family, she said that too. And I want to, Sue, I really do, I want that with her too, but, I don't know how we . . . you know . . . how do we do that? What should I say to Mum, Sue?"

Susan did not laugh. He had been afraid she would laugh, but she did not. This was a relief, and a good sign for George, he must have explained it to her in the right way; she was taking him seriously. Susan lowered her head and sighed, staring at her hands which were clutched together in front of her. Her elbows were on her knees, and she was leaning forward, sitting on her computer chair, balancing, so she looked as though she would fall forwards if he nudged her. George was on her bed sitting on his hands.

He waited through her sighs and the silence, she was bound to say something if he waited for long enough. Finally Susan sighed for the last time, shook her head, and looked up at him.

"You've no idea have you, George?"

"What do you mean?" he answered, "I love her, and she loves me."

"No, I mean about Mum and Dad . . . and everyone else for that matter. They're never going to let two Downs like you set up and live together."

She sat up, and started waving her arm around making sweeping gestures towards the window as she spoke.

"You're disabled, George, and so is she, you can't have kids or anything. How would you live, George? You don't have money; you can't look after a whole house. This is just a dream, you can't do stuff like that . . . not really, no one will let you. Christ, it would be like if you said you wanted to marry her or something! George, you never really got it did you?"

At this point Susan leaned right forward again and tried to look at him, her gaze intent, her voice low and powerful.

"Why you go to that stupid centre, why you go to College and play on a Pumpkin computer instead of a proper one like mine. Being disabled like you are, it's more than not being able to read, George, it means you're different, you can't do stuff like the rest of us. Why do you think you have a social worker? I don't have a social worker do I? You do because you need one, because you're disabled, you have a learning disability, haven't you even learned that much?"

George sat and gazed at a space somewhere through Susan's head. He had been looking at her and then he had started thinking and lost focus. He had tried to let her words wash over him, but then she had said that one word and everything she said after that had washed right passed him. It had hit him like a punch to the stomach, that one word, moved him to his core. She was right of course, so right; he should ask Tracy to marry him! It was the only thing to do. If they were going to live together, and they were so in love, of course they should get married.

George's mind was racing, working out what he would have to do. He would have to get a ring for her, a beautiful ring, the right one. Susan had said something about money, she was right about this too; he really did not have any money. How was he going to get a ring with no money? And where would he propose to Tracy?

He knew he had to do it right, get down on one knee, he had seen it on the TV. He had to wear a suit and tie, get down on one knee and give her a ring.

He looked up and realised Susan was still talking, George had not heard a word she had said for a while, and he really wanted to get out now, go upstairs and think. It had been such a huge day, he needed to lie down and think it all through properly. He waited for Susan to stop talking.

"OK, yes, thanks, Sue, thank you. Yes." He got up and went to open the door. "See you later."

"What?" he turned round startled by her shout. Susan was staring at him incredulously.

"Is that it? I just tell you all that and you say thank you and leave? Is that it? Is that all you're going to say?"

"Well, yeh. Susan I need to go . . . you know . . . and lie down to think OK? Can we talk about it later? Maybe tomorrow?"

"Whatever," she snapped and turned away. George left.

Susan sat and looked out of the window thinking about George and what had just happened. She had never talked to George like that before. She had never really talked to him about being disabled at all. She knew he was a Downs of course, she'd always known that, but they had never talked about it.

When George had come in and said he wanted to move in with his girlfriend she had felt frightened for him. Mum was going to kill him! She was amazed he did not know how Mum would react. Why did he not know he would never be able to do anything like that? Was he really that thick? Had no one ever told him? Mum had told him he was special, she knew that. "Too special for Comprehensive school", "too special to go straight to College from home", "too special to get a job". She had heard Mum saying these things to him all her life, but what did *he* think it meant?

Susan started to cry. She did not really know why, what it was about, she had just taken a risk and told George outright that he was disabled, what she knew it meant and he had just walked out and left her. She had thought it would be the start of a conversation. She had thought he would argue with her, say that he could do anything he wanted disabled or not, or something . . . anything. But he had just walked out and left her there.

She was angry with him for leaving her like that. The more she thought about it now, the more worried she got. Why had he left? Had she upset him so much? Was he up there on his own really upset because of what she said? Perhaps he had never realised he could not do stuff like that, she had told him straight out and perhaps he just could not cope with hearing the truth like that.

Susan sat for some time getting more and more worried about George and what she had said to him. She needed to know whether he was all right or not, so she did what she had never done before; she went and knocked on his bedroom door when it was shut.

"George?" Sue's voice echoed softly around the room. She heard him move in the bed, as she reached the top of the stairs he was leaning up on one elbow facing her.

"It's OK, Sue, cummon up. Are you OK?"

"God yeh! I'm fine, I was worried about you, are you OK? You left so quickly after I said all that . . . stuff . . . to you, I've been worrying. I'm sorry I upset you like that, I've never seen you upset like that . . . just walking out. What's going on with you?"

George sat up in bed, and she sat on it with him.

"Oh, well, I'm thinking you know? This whole thing, I mean, living with Tracy, it's all a bit, you know? . . . "

"Yeh. Huge. God, I don't know what I'd do if anyone asked me to move in with them."

"But it's not like anyone, you know? It's Tracy. I love her so much, Sue, I really want this. What you said, I think you're right, I think . . . "

"No, that's what I came to try and talk about, I don't think I am right. I think I was wrong to say that to you."

"You do? You don't think I should?"

"Oh, George I don't know. Really, I don't know what you should or shouldn't do. I just know it'll be really hard for you. But, I don't think that's very fair. At all. It's just true."

"Yeh, maybe you're right, Sue, maybe I should just leave it for a bit."

"Why don't you talk to Tracy some more, see what she thinks? She's like you isn't she? So she'll know as well as you do, she might have a plan?"

"She had this paper . . . you know? Someone called Tim I think, it said he could help us. She's gonna ring him. Probably that's better, it's her idea. She knows more than me about, well, you know, lots of stuff."

He paused and they both gazed at the bed clothes in front of them. Susan was waiting for him to say something else, she could not just leave yet, but she could think of nothing helpful to say. She could see she had said something wrong, he looked up and she hoped he would say something that could make it all right.

"It's all too much at once you know? That's why I left your room then. I just need to think and try and sort it out. I wasn't upset you know? I just had to lie down and be OK."

George lay back down, so Susan got up to leave.

"You OK?"

"OK, well, you know, all right. Thanks for coming to see me."

She felt her way gingerly back down the stairs in the dark and went straight back to the game.

*   *   *

Oemor was falling. He was in a narrow, vertical tunnel and he was falling. There was no sign of landing at all. He realised that all the air rushing past him and movement was distracting him from thinking very clearly.

What on earth was going on?

Oemor felt a sense of panic as he sped past the rock face, he was falling very quickly now, his arms were flailing around uncontrollably and he knew he was going to land, hard and all too soon. Oemor braced himself well, but did not think he could survive the impact. Why had he not got his c-cylinder out?

He realised that it had not been a pointless thing to do, it was an essential thing to do, clearly he had saved himself the first time by breaking his fall. Why could he not move in the same way this time? He did not seem to be able to control himself. He was braced for landing and had been for some time before it came. Oemor felt the rock on his feet, the impact shook through his legs, his torso and up through his skull.

He lay still, wondering vaguely if he was any shorter than before. There should be a dent in the rock, where his body was imbedded in the surface. His heartbeat rang through him and the rock surrounding him making the whole tunnel feel alive.

He tried to get up, but found himself flailing around, out of control. Although gradually his movements became more deliberate, more controlled, he felt shocked and frightened to not know what his body was doing. He eventually managed to sit up, falling over backwards a few times to begin with, but then Oemor felt his body slow its movements down and carefully, steadily learn how to sit up properly. He was stricken with a contained panic, unable to do anything different, unable to control anything.

After an hour Oemor had learned how to stand and hold his balance. He had figured out a careful, methodical pattern to how his body was learning to control itself, and in the end he was able to stand firm and look around. His head eventually came to an unsteady rest facing the cave entrance he had previously rolled so smoothly into. He was sure this was back at the beginning and so he knew that if he did not get going now the Nephillim would be coming up into this cave and would be standing still, invisible, waiting for him to walk right into them.

Worst of all, he had no knowledge of Susan. He had become increasingly aware of Susan, her thoughts and feelings, as he had gone on through the tunnels. He knew she had a vivid imagination – even though she was trapped in a cave she was thinking about school and whether anyone liked her. Oemor loved her so much and had been feeling so close and bonded to her, to suddenly be back at the beginning of the cave, with no knowledge of her at all in his mind was a huge loss. All he had now was his memory. He ached for her, he felt terrible that he was suddenly so far away, when he had been getting closer to rescuing her. What would she think? Where had he gone wrong?

Walking proved to be harder than he thought, he stumbled, reeled around and tumbled over, rolling head over heels into the tunnel.

Oemor came to a smooth rest just by the shimmering rock where he knew the gun was. He found he could control the roll much more this time and had not hurt himself at all. This was good as he badly needed first aid for most of his body after the impact of the fall, and he only had one on him. He should use it now; he knew he would pick another one up later. He needed to get the gun and ammo that was in the rock just next to him. He got up, and started walking again. Much slower and much more carefully, as though he was learning to walk for the first time. Oemor walked slowly and carefully away from the only gun he had ever found in the caves, away from the bullets he so badly needed, and away from the first aid kit he needed to heal his aching body.

Oemor was screaming inside, his body was being forced to do something he had no wish to do. He was frightened of going any further without the gun, and felt a rising panic worse than before. Not being able to walk or control his body properly had unnerved him, but this was terrible. His heartbeat remained steady and calm, but his mind was filling with a flood of horror and lack of control. He used this fear, and used all his strength, to resist walking away from the gun. He pushed against his own legs to stop them from moving forwards, he pulled at his torso to turn himself round. He was frightened and fighting an inner battle. His heart was beating fast and loud in his chest, his mind was pushing with all his strength and willpower to go back. He finally felt himself turn slightly in the right direction. The single, slight movement swept through him with a wave of surprise, he pushed harder against whatever was holding him back.

It was working, slowly Oemor was taking control of his own body. He turned his own body round, wrenching himself through a great physical power, working against his own body to move in a different way. He forced himself back to the rock, pushing all the way, he was figuring out how to work around this, how to push past his legs and bring them with him. He felt as though he was being stretched out along the whole cave, as though part of him stayed where he had turned round, pulling his body out in a line to get that gun. He made it . . . he was there. He had to bend down, which was harder than he had thought, but he was starting to get the hang of it now. He pushed his hand forward. At this point whatever had been holding him back snapped through him, back into him, whole, and started to help. Oemor did not know what was going on, but he reached in and got the gun and the ammo as fast as his clumsy movements would let him.

His pulse went right up at the sight of the gun, which was odd. He was so used to it, he had been down here for days, and the gun felt like an essential part of him. It was something to feel relieved and comforted by, not this fear and wonder that was washing over him now.

As Oemor tried to set off again in the right direction, fully armed, he felt renewed, as though he had won a great battle. As he moved clumsily, almost dropping the gun and unable to put his ammo away, he realised he might have a double fight on his hands, the Nephillim and his own body at the same time.

*   *   *

Since Christmas Susan had done nothing outside school but play on her computer. She would think about ammo packs during maths, finding it easy to work out subtraction in terms of bullets used and available, rather than just the numbers on the paper. In English reading Shakespeare's sonnets they made sense as Oemor's love for her in the game, in religious studies she knew Oemor was sacrificing himself for love, and in games she ran faster if she pretended to hold a gun and escape flesh-eating giants than just jogging along the tow-path.

Her hand felt the joystick during school, like her head still felt a hat after she had taken it off. When she got in she ran straight upstairs just to feel the beating of her heart in his before she could take her coat off. Susan was in front of her computer, joystick in hand, headphones on, unwashed and unresponsive, for the whole weekend every weekend.

She spent almost as much time writing in the journal as actually playing the game. Filling it in each day felt interesting and helped her a lot. If she came to Oemor, who loved her, she could tell him anything. She knew he was fighting to rescue her, risking himself and also strangely needing her to help him rescue her. It was all a bit mixed up in her head, but she felt closely connected to Oemor, and felt when she was playing the game that he loved her. He was brave and determined, she was convinced she could feel more than just his heart beating. When her hand was on the joystick properly she could feel the full extent of his love, courage and desperation. It did not seem to matter to him that she was nasty to everyone else, so she told him everything, and he loved her completely.

Susan fell into bed very late. She had stayed up playing the game past two in the morning every night that week and now she knew she was really good at it. She drifted off into a much-needed sleep, and dreamt she was in the Nephillim caves. She was searching for something, but was not sure what. Something she needed to find. Searching through the caves and crying out loud in a voice frustratingly weak, she emerged without warning into an opening just like one of the large caverns in the game. She paused to look round and noticed shimmering areas of rock face on the far side. She knew what she was looking for was there, so she ran towards the far wall. Halfway there, in the centre of the cave, she saw a bright, white light above her. She stopped, looked up and saw an angel floating down directly above her. She stumbled backwards to make room but it did not land. Susan could clearly see its feet about two metres off the ground, even the toenails were there to see. Do angels cut their toenails? That was an image that made her smile as she leaned back to see the figure properly.

It bent over slightly and looked down at her. It smiled and she weakly smiled back. A voice sounded in her mind although the angel's mouth did not move.

"Susan," it said, "look for the feet, Susan."

What? She had been looking at its feet, what was it talking about?

"Susan," it repeated almost the same words, "Shoot for the feet."

Susan glanced towards the wall of the cave on the other side, beyond the angel, remembering she had been searching for something. As she looked back the angel disappeared, leaving no trace of light in the green caves. She ran across the rest of the cavern and reached into the first hole she had seen.

What she pulled out made her body jolt as she slept. In the dream she screamed and backed away from what she saw. It was unmistakeably George's severed hand. It was not just anyone's hand, this was clearly George's – his were different. She moved slowly, filled with horror to the next opening in the rock face, and hardly dared to look at what she pulled out.

It was George's head.

Susan woke with a start, sitting up. What on earth? She looked around the room in confusion and panic. The room was dark and quiet, starkly normal. It was a dream, just a dream, she lay back down, relaxing. She breathed out deeply with relief, as her heartbeat slowed she fell back into a calm, dreamless sleep.

Chapter 4

George was nervous as they went into the room, he glanced shyly at Tracy, wanting to hold hands. His hands were sweating and he thought Tracy would not like that. Tracy looked worried and he knew they had been told off many times for holding hands. He did not want to get off to a bad start.

"Hi you two, George is it? And you must be Tracy? Hi, hi, come in, come in, take a pew."

The young man grinned and shook them vigorously by the hand, then gestured for them to sit down. The room was a light, bright office space, with desk and chair positioned to catch the best light. A sofa and two chairs had been squeezed into one corner, along with a tiny coffee table, box of tissues, and a plant. The brightness of the room, provided by large windows and a winter sun, made the space seem larger than it was.

George and Tracy went straight for the sofa and sat close to each other. George leaned forward and sat on his hands, staring at the ground. Tracy sat back into the cushions with her arms crossed and her hands secured in her armpits.

"My name is Tim, I know we haven't met before but I spoke to you, Tracy, on the phone didn't I?" Tracy nodded.

"Yes, and I understand the two of you have been going out with each other for some time and now you want to move into a house together by yourselves? Is that right?"

They both nodded and George did not dare to look at him. Was he going to laugh? Tell them they were not allowed to? Separate them? The fear of what he could do to them was stifling.

"Right, well, as I said to you on the phone, Tracy, I can try and explain to you what might be involved in you doing that, let you know where to go and who you need to talk to. Basically the more support you have from family and friends the easier, and quicker, this is going to be. I must warn you though, this isn't going to be easy, for either of you, and it is certainly going to take some time."

"How long is 'some time'?" Tracy asked.

"Well, that depends on a lot of different things, Tracy, what benefits you'll be able to get, how much rent you can claim and what housing stock there is available amongst others. If all goes well and both your families are supportive I should think you could be moving in together some time next year."

Tracy looked up.

"But, it's only January now," she said, "that means *all* of this year before 'some time' next year?"

George's head was hung low, his chin almost on his chest. He was frowning, though no one could tell his face was so hidden.

"I know, I know, it seems far away." Tim said "I can see from your faces that you're disappointed . . . " Tim leaned forward tipping his chair towards them, " . . . and I must be honest, that's an optimistic view, if all goes well."

"Why?" George was still staring at the ground two feet in front of him.

"Pardon?" Tim started slightly, up until now he had been talking just to Tracy.

"Why so long?" George looked up, his eyes wide, his face showing nothing but curiosity. "We moved at home you know? And it took seven months, all four of us, and a new school for Sue and a new job for Mum. There's only the two of us, you know? We haven't got jobs, or schools, or anything. And we don't have to wait to sell any house like Mum and Dad, we can move now. We want to move in, now."

Tim held George's gaze for a while, till his head dropped, his eyes studying his own feet.

"George," Tim's head shook from side to side as he spoke, "You may not have a job, but that means you have no income, so you can't just buy a house like your . . . "

"No what?"

"Pardon?"

Tracy and George spoke simultaneously.

"I have no what?" George carried on, "You said I have no in-what?"

"No income." Tim said, "It means money, George, you don't earn any money, so you can't buy a house like your Mum and Dad did. You have to claim your rent out of your money, which I think probably goes to your Mum and Dad at the moment. That's why it will be quicker and easier with support from your families. I assume your parents are all right about all of this?"

George looked sideways at Tracy, who shook her head slightly and looked away. They said nothing.

"For both of you," Tim said, "I mean, how did they take it when you told them? Are your families all right about you setting up home together? They do know, don't they?"

In the silence that followed George's heart sank. He thought now that Susan had been trying to protect him from doing this, because she knew, and now he realised, Mum and Dad were going to shout a lot – an awful lot – about this. It would not be all right with them at all. Of course he would have to tell them, and of course they were going to be angry with him. He had somehow hoped they could do it without Mum and Dad knowing. Of course that was ridiculous. This whole thing was ridiculous.

George flushed and sank lower into the sofa. He was never going to be able to do this.

"OK."

Tim's words echoed round the silence in the room. He had said it in a long and drawn out way, as though he was saying 'Aha, I see, like that is it? This is going to be harder than I had first thought'.

George looked up and gave Tim a thin, sheepish smile.

George surprised himself, and spoke first.

"My Mum and Dad, you know? I haven't told them. I don't know, you know? They won't like it. I think she'll shout. Mum shouts you see, so, I don't know. And, I'm not sure about the money, you know? You said I have some but she gets it? I don't know about that. But I think she'll shout, my Mum. Sue said I was disabled and couldn't do things like this. She was annoyed, but she came up later, you know, to my room, and she said she was sorry, you know, for saying that. So maybe Mum will shout and then do that, say sorry afterwards, you know?"

George sat back on the sofa and breathed out heavily. It was more than he was used to saying at once.

Tracy turned to him, saying,

"I didn't know your Mum shouted, George" at the same time as Tim said

"I'm sorry, who's Sue, George?"

George heard them both saying, "I'm didn't sorry know Sue shouted George" and they had to wait while he sat bewildered and heard each sentence through again in his head.

"Sue's my sister," George replied to Tim. He knew he could talk to Tracy another time about his Mum.

"Oh, I see," Tim was nodding "OK. So you have told your sister. Is she older than you?"

"Younger. Fourteen years younger."

"Oh. OK. And she said you couldn't live together because you're disabled?" George nodded, hanging his head again. He was embarrassed about the word 'disabled'. He had heard it enough times in his life. He was sure it was something he should feel bad about, but he was not sure how to make it stop. He knew if he could he would.

"Well, she's wrong about that, George," Tim leant forward and tried to catch George's eye, "People who are disabled like you can get your own house and live together, you certainly can. I have helped people do it, and I can help the two of you as well. It's important that you know that you can do this. What your sister said, Sue, is it?"

"Susan," George corrected him. He knew how much Sue hated anyone else calling her Sue.

"Right, well what Susan is getting at is that it is harder for people who are disabled. I know it shouldn't be . . . " he said to Tracy, hearing her take a breath, " . . . but the reality of the situation is that it will be harder for you two than it would be for another young couple wanting to set up home together."

George visibly flushed at being called a 'young couple', he looked at Tracy and reached for her hand. He could see her flushing too and the look she gave him was loving embarrassment. George saw Tim notice them holding hands and he held his breath waiting to see if he would tell them to stop. He did not tell them to stop; in fact he made no comment at all, but a huge smile spread across Tim's face. This was his only reaction. George liked him for that, and held Tracy's hand in his for the rest of the session.

"And . . . " Tim carried on where he left off " . . . it will, like I said, be harder if your families are not going to support you one hundred percent. There's not only the actual process you have to go through, which I can help you with as much as you need, but there's also the potential for social stigmatism, which you may face wherever you decide to live."

"What?" George asked.

"There's the what for what? You can't say stuff like that with us, Tim," Tracy said, "We're Downs you know, you said it yourself. You have to explain things to us so we both understand. Otherwise we can't work with you. Don't use big words, say it so we can get it OK?"

"Oh God! Of course, I'm sorry, I got carried away. You're right, of course, Tracy, I'm sorry." Tim held up both his hands as he was talking, as though he was surrendering to them in a cowboy movie.

"Thank you, both of you, I'll do my best. It's really good for you to . . . erm . . . check that out. You must, of course, always tell me if I say anything you don't understand. I mean, I know you just did, and thanks, and it's really important that you always do that. Sorry. Right. Thanks."

Taking a breath, Tim carried on,

"OK, yes. What I mean is that if you get a house somewhere and your neighbours don't want to live next to you. They might not want you to move in. Or you might get robbed more often if people know you are disabled, or you might get bullied, you know, picked on more, if you don't live at home. Do you see what I mean now?"

George nodded, and felt Tracy nodding next to him as well, he felt sad. They both knew what Tim was talking about now, and he had never thought about that at all.

As the meeting went on George realised more and more how little he had really thought about this. He felt as though he had thought of nothing else, but sitting here on Tim's sofa in this bright office, the reality of it started to sink in. It started to sound impossible, it felt as though he had had a dream, a romantic, unrealistic, silly dream that everyone else knew could never happen.

George felt a little foolish, almost ashamed, that he could have believed that living together was something that they could do. He had only been thinking about them being in a house together, cooking, cleaning, looking after each other, maybe even having a baby, perhaps getting a job as a chef to help with money, Tracy getting a job with computers or something, maybe. These were the details he had been thinking about all the time, and these daydreams had brought him so much joy. Now he was faced with the reality of getting the house in the first place. George realised how much there was to do, and how little he knew about any of it. The whole thing overwhelmed him.

Tim realised that this new couple had become sadder and deflated the longer they had been with him. The more realistic and practical he tried to be, the further into the sofa they sank, their faces low, eyes down. He had thought it was important for them to know that what they wanted to do would be hard, but he did not want them to give up. It was never easy for him to help people get a house together, but it was so much harder without parental support. His heart sank. Tim was also feeling disappointed.

When he had spoken to Tracy on the phone she had seemed to be pretty with it. Tim had hoped they would be an able and capable couple who he would be able to support well. He really wanted to support people well in getting what they wanted. So far he had never managed it smoothly. Tim had hoped they would be a couple he could really do something with.

He got out a large sheet of paper and some big felt pens and spread them out on the coffee table, moving the tissues and plant onto the floor beside him. They both leant forward watching him now with their full attention. Tim had seen this happen before, when he was just talking with people after a while they would glaze over, as though thinking about something else. Getting out pens and paper in the middle of a meeting was a sure way to get someone's attention.

"Right," Tim took the lid off one of the pens with a satisfying popping noise, and the room filled with the smell of pear drops, "One thing that is always clear, for all of us, is that you can't go through something like this on your own. You're going to need a lot of help. That's not about you, that's just the way of the world. I needed a lot of help to move into a new house with my girlfriend. So, what I want to do is I'm going to see if I can get an idea of the people in your lives, who's important to you, how close people are to you, and who may be able to help you get what you want in your lives, OK?"

"I can't read."

"No, I know, it's OK," Tim held up his hand, "I'm going to try and draw pictures on the sheet, so we can all see it and we can all understand together, would that be all right George?"

Tim looked directly at George when he asked him this. It was the first time George had looked right at him. He was struck by the clear blueness of George's eyes, large and bright with curiosity. George stared down at the paper, and shrugged.

"No writing though," he said.

"No writing," nodded Tim, and he drew two people like they were cartoons in the middle of the sheet. He drew them holding hands, and he said, "This is the two of you, then, here in the middle."

Tim was smiling as he drew, Tracy and George watched and grinned, leaning forward in their chairs, and started telling him what to draw. They pointed at the sheet and named people, showing him how close they felt, and pointing out physical features for Tim to include so they could recognise who was who.

When they had finished Tim sat back on his ankles and looked at them. They seemed happy, highlighting for themselves the people they wanted to help them move. Maybe, he wondered, just maybe this would be the one he could feel proud of.

*   *   *

Susan jumped and let go of the joystick in her surprise. That was odd. She had started the game so many times, she had never felt such a sudden rush of fear. As she took a grip on the joystick again she felt calm, and a strange sense of relief. This made no sense to Susan at all, he was in exactly the same spot as he had been before. The same cave, low on rations, high on ammo, with a clear path in front of him, ready to set off.

As she settled down to play the game Susan thought she needed to know a bit more about this new learning program she was playing with, now that she had got the hang of the game. She had also started to wonder whether they had spent so long programming the character that they had missed out on developing the game itself. She realised that if it had not been for the gaming journal and the way the joystick made her feel she would be getting bored with it by now.

Susan played for a little while, but she had been a little unnerved by the different emotional hit and as soon as it was after six o'clock she stopped playing so that she could go on the Internet.

Absolutely everyone else had broadband now, but of course Mum and Dad would not pay for that, so she had to wait and use the phone line. It was cheaper after six in the evening, so that was the only time she was allowed to use it. She went straight to the *CP4You* website, which just had adverts for her computer, and links for people who had bought earlier computers. There was not an upgrade for hers yet . . . it really was brand new. Susan was very happy to see this, Mum and Dad really had got the best present this time. She saw a link to the *Nephillim Caves* website which she clicked on. This was more like what she was looking for.

The site had been written by one of the games programmers and the marketing department. It was created to look like a pirate site, and it had a page on 'Hints and Tips for Better Play'. As she scrolled down through the fighting tips, game play strategies and extra hidden food supply tips, Susan was overjoyed to find that she already knew all of them. She was feeling pretty smug by the time she found an explanation about how to save valuable life points by using the c-cylinder to break the initial fall. She really was good at this game.

Susan had a good browse around the site and was about to give up – she had not read anything she did not already know – when she saw a small link in blue print at the bottom of the 'So you think you're a Nephillim Annihilator' page. It said, 'Get more stuff'. She clicked on it and it took her to an online gaming shop. Susan had never been that interested in these before, she had never known how to buy anything over the Internet. This page was selling 'pre-release-date gaming extras' and had what was called 'The *Nephillim Caves* master com'. The photograph looked like headphones with a small microphone attached, which bent round to the mouth on a small plastic stick. It also had the *Nephillim Caves* logo on, exactly the same as the logo on the joystick. Susan skimmed through the information until she found the phrase she was looking for – 'using the same interactive technology, newly developed and exclusive to CP4You'.

That was it, Susan knew she just had to have one of those, it looked as though it would mean she could talk to Oemor. All she had to do was work out how to get it. Susan had never really had spare money of her own. The pocket money she got was for her regular spending, she didn't have any left at the end of the week. To buy something new she would have to go without something. Susan decided to take her usual first course of action in this situation – she would just ask Mum for the money. This was more than she was used to asking for so she knew it was going to be hard, she thought it would make her Mum shout quite a bit. She decided that she would do something nice, so that Mum would feel happy with her before she asked her for money. She decided to go and offer to help with cooking the evening meal.

*   *   *

What Susan did not realise was how little money her parents actually had, and that earning enough to keep her and George at home and happy meant that they were both working long hours in jobs they did not really like. This made both her parents feel unhappy, and so when they were at home, they were unhappy with the people around them. This was made much worse when they saw Susan not applying herself to school at all, and getting low-grade results. Susan was clearly intelligent and they could see that she could do so much more, if only she tried.

For Susan's Mum it was worse. Susan's Mum was angry . . . really angry. Somewhere inside her where she had barely even thought about it, Susan's Mum was angry with her because Susan could do everything that George could not, and she was wasting it. Susan's

Mum had watched George grow up, discovered with him everything that he could not do, realised after him how that made people treat him, and it had broken her heart.

She had been devastated when they had told her George was abnormal.

She had felt worse when they told her he had Downs Syndrome. She knew what that was, her sister had called him a 'Mongol' and she had slammed the phone down on her. Bringing up a child like that had broken Susan's mother from the inside out. She had found it mortifying. She had always been popular and fitted in, right through her childhood, and into sixth-form college, when George had been born. Being pregnant had not been so bad; it was considered an odd kind of cool. Most of the kids who were pregnant at seventeen did not go into the sixth form, they left school to get married and raise families.

George's Mum had had great plans for herself. She found studying hard, but liked it when she got the right answers, and had been genuinely interested in most of her subjects. She had planned to go on and make something of herself. She was going to be the first person in her family to get a degree. She was going to take a year out before going to University and travel around Europe. She had had plans. And then there was George. She had loved George with all her heart, mind and body, from the day she felt him kick inside her. She was happy to give up all those plans to have George, to love him, and to raise him right.

Then he had been born. While her stitches healed, she had stayed in hospital, and the nurses had given her strange smiles and stayed more distant than from the other young Mums. The Doctor had been typically stoical.

"Well, from the look of your son Miss Eckert, I think we need to get some tests done. We won't be able to confirm anything for the first few weeks. Obviously, we can't go just on an observational diagnosis with a boy like this, so the sooner we can get him tested the sooner we'll know where to go from here."

Susan's Mum did not know what he meant. She had been sent home and that had been that. Three months later, after everyone in the street had looked at George and said,

"Oh, you poor thing," or looked uncomfortable and turned away, the midwife came round and told her to make an appointment with her family doctor. He shuffled papers and pretended to read a report before he peered up at her, smiled, tipped his head to the one side, and said,

"I'm sorry to have to tell you, Miss Eckert, your son has Downs Syndrome. I'm sure you had realised by now that there was something different about him, and it's clear from these test results that this is what it is."

"You mean . . . what does that mean? He's going to be retarded?" She had not used that word since then. She had been eighteen, it was the only word she had known, right there and then in front of the doctor. Still, it was such an ugly, damning word, she felt shame that she had ever said it.

"Well, yes, Miss Eckert, that is what it means, although that is an older term for it. We don't tend to use words like that any more. He is disabled though. This is a serious matter for you, and you are very young, so I'm going to see if I can find some kind of group or support service for you, OK?" He had looked down then and she was not sure if she should leave.

"But, I don't know what this means."

"What this means, Miss Eckert, is that your son will never gain full adulthood. He may not be able to read or write, although some do, but he will need to be looked after for the rest of his life. It's important that you recognise this, Miss Eckert. You will be looking after George now for the rest of your life. He is never going to really grow up." He never looked up, he never looked at her for the rest of the conversation, his eyes wandered around his desk and book case, but he never looked at her.

"Now, it is possible for George to be taken somewhere where he'll be properly looked after. You'll be able to see him as much as you want, but it means that George would not be the life-long burden to you that he will be if you choose to keep him at home."

George's Mum had later found out that what the doctor told her was not true, not only about the support, but also about the kind of care available. At the time she could not think of anything but that he had wanted to take George away from her. She had picked him up and walked out there and then. As she turned away from the GP and away from the support he was offering her, she realised that nothing mattered to her, nothing, other than that she kept George with her. If it meant looking after him until she died then that is what she would do; but nothing else mattered, she had to have George with her.

And so she had. And she had got on, raised George until he had gone to his special kind of school. Then she had got on and got a job, got on and met Susan's Dad, got on and married, and eventually they had got on and had another child. George's Mum knew that this time everything would be different, everything would be right and maybe Susan would go to university, maybe Susan would be the first in their family to get a degree, maybe Susan would take a year out and travel round Europe.

Susan's Mum could see by the time she went to comprehensive school that Susan was brighter than her Mum had ever been. Susan did not find studying hard at all, she could do it all, and do it easily. She could also see that Susan was not interested in what she was supposed to be learning. Susan was bored, and then Susan started to mess up. The lowering grades had been one thing, but when she had started hanging around with a group of kids from the estate who skipped classes, Susan's Mum got angry.

So, Mum and Dad had sat down together and talked it through. They had gone through their finances and gone to their bank and they had made decisions and they moved the family across town. They had worked it out so that George could still go to the same day centre, but Susan had to change school. It would mean Mum would have to work longer hours, and Dad would have to move to a promotion he did not want that paid him more money. They had planned it all so that Susan would be able to concentrate on school, she would find new friends who liked their school, and she would study hard.

It should have been a good plan, and could probably have worked. The only real mistake they made was not actually explaining the plan to Susan. So, when Susan decided to ask her Mum for some money to buy the *Nephillim Caves* master com over the Internet, she did not know what she was walking into at all: she thought she was just trying to get some money from her Mum, who she had been rude to for the last few months.

*   *   *

George came home from the meeting with Tim with such a confusing mixture of emotions that he went straight upstairs to lie down. He needed to lie on his bed, watch the clouds drift past and think through what had been said. He was determined that he was going to tell his Mum and Dad tonight about wanting to move in with Tracy. He just needed to think carefully about what he was going to say. He went straight past the kitchen door, where he could hear Susan was home already and talking to Mum; he could tell Mum was not happy, but he paid very little attention. This was not unusual and he needed to work things out in his head.

George was disappointed to realise that it was dark outside, he was later than usual, and he could not see the clouds. He had imagined being able to lie down and gaze at the blue sky, watch the white clouds going pink as the sun set out of sight. When he got home from the centre at this time of year he could do that almost every night. Tonight he was later than usual, there had been a hold up on the bus.

It was also a bit too cold in his room for lying out on top of the bed. It had been a cold wintry day, and the attic room was difficult to keep warm. George got in under the covers and lay on his side, huddled round in a foetal position, clutching the covers under his neck to keep the warmth in. His eyes did not focus on anything in particular. Although he was troubled by the day and had lots to think about, George drifted into a light sleep. The night sky cleared above his head, stars came out and shone through his window, and George floated off into a dream.

He dreamt about Susan's computer game. He was in one of the caves, running, looking for something, then ran out into a huge cavern, as vast as a cathedral, with a ceiling so high he could hardly see it. As he was looking up he saw a bright light above him, which floated down and as it floated down in front of him the image of an angel became clear within the bright, white light. The angel bent over slightly and looked down at him. It smiled and he smiled back. The voice sounded inside his mind . . . the angel's mouth did not move at all.

"George" it said, "look for the feet, George."

George did not know what that meant, but he did not say anything, he just smiled and watched as the angel rose up, floated high into the top of the cavern, and disappeared. He stood still for a while and looked around the cavern. He saw the rock shimmering on the opposite side and went over to see what was in there. Reaching his hand in he found something cold and cylindrical. He pulled it out; it was made of heavy brushed metal, about ten inches long, and two inches wide.

George woke softly and lay still, remembering the dream, how beautiful the angel had looked, what it had said, how the sound of its voice had resonated in his mind, not from its mouth. He thought it was a beautiful dream, and he thought he would tell Susan about it tonight, as well as telling Mum and Dad about wanting to live with Tracy. His stomach turned somersaults at this thought, and he got out of bed to go and get ready for the meal to come. He decided that he would do something nice for his Mum, so that she would feel happy with him before he told her; he decided to go and offer to help with cooking the meal.

Chapter 5

Afterwards in the Sarandon household the meal was always referred to as That Damn Meal. They would say,

"It was That Damn Meal when it all started you know, none of this would have happened without that" or,

"It's That Damn Meal you know, I can't eat chicken now without thinking about it."

When Susan's Mum sat down to start the meal she was feeling annoyed with Susan, sorry for herself and ashamed of her husband. This in itself was not unusual, all of her resentment and anger at Susan had been seeping out around the edges of her interactions more and more lately, she had been feeling slightly out of control with how she was treating her own family.

Over the past few months Susan's Mum knew she had been snapping at Susan and not treating her very well; they both seemed to have got hooked in to being like that with each other. This evening, the evening of That Damn Meal, Susan had come down early and offered to help with the food. This had surprised her Mum, a kind offer from Susan!

She did not know what to do other than say yes . . . it would be just too rude to say no, and she really had needed a hand. She had decided to do a roast, and she had forgotten how many things there are to do and how crucial the timing was with roast dinners. She had read in one of her magazines that 'A quick and easy answer to those mid-week blues' was to 'Roast a bird the easy way'.

She had got a chicken cheap on the market, but when she got home she could not find the magazine again. She could not even remember where exactly she had been when she read it, and the realisation that it had probably been at the hairdressers, not at home, had sunk steadily into her stomach. She had spent so long looking for the recipe, it was getting late, and eventually she cooked the chicken the only way she knew how, the way her mother had cooked roasts on Sundays; traditionally, and with all the trimmings.

This took longer, and was more complicated than she was used to for a weekday meal and she was actually relieved at the offer of help, however unusual it was. The only reason she hesitated was because she did not trust her daughter. They had been bickering with each other for months now; why would she suddenly offer some help?

Susan turned out to be very useful in the kitchen, she listened to what she was told to do and then got on and did it . . . she was cheerful and did not get in the way. Mrs Sarandon was confused by this and fumbled around for a while not knowing what to do until she knocked a chopping board full of raw, partly chopped carrots onto the floor.

"Fuckinell."

"It's all right Mum, I'll clear that up."

They both looked up as they heard George coming downstairs. Mum thought he must have thought she had shouted for dinner, and she looked up sheepishly when he came in. Susan was on her knees picking carrots up off the floor and putting them back onto the chopping board, Mrs Sarandon was standing leaning on the worktop feeling tired, and dinner was clearly not ready.

"I know how to cut carrots," he said, "I could do those for you, I'm good at cooking, one of the best."

He grinned at Susan and she winked back at him. Their Mum watched this exchange with a bewildered passivity. Both of them? Helping? How did they know?

She watched as Susan rinsed the carrots off and gave them to him with the board, knife and a clear space for him to work. She saw George grin again as he took the knife.

George with a knife? Mrs Sarandon had never seen George use a knife, she had always been too frightened of him cutting himself, she thought he would never have been able to do anything without hurting himself. She hesitated, and in that hesitation she watched her son smile as he took hold of a knife, hold a carrot like chefs do on the television, and chop a carrot. It was one fluid, efficient

64

movement. Then he picked up the board and swept the orange pieces into the saucepan, take another carrot and do it again. Tears welled in her eyes as she stood and saw him doing something she had never let him do.

"George, where did you? . . . How did you?" She paused.

Susan came back in and pushed past her to check the potatoes on the hob.

"George goes to College, Mum, to learn to cook, you remember? That meeting you went to, they said he was going to College for a cooking class. It's been two years now, he's bound to have picked up a few tricks, isn't that right George?"

"Yes, I can cook well, Mum, I'm the best in the class." George gave her the same smile he gave her when he used to play football with Mr Sarandon. Adam would let him score a goal and George would run towards her saying "I'm the best footballer Mum, I'm the best!" Adam had not played football with George since they had married, she realised he had only been doing it to impress her. It had worked, he was the only man she had gone out with who made any effort to get on with George at all. It had been a big part of what she had loved about him then.

George's Mum had always thought that the tutors at College did the same thing, they 'let' George cook, just as Adam had let him score a goal and allowed him to believe he was good at football. Watching him now she realised that George really did know what he was doing, he was not going to cut himself at all . . . he was better at this than she was.

"Well, yes, OK, George, I can see you are really good at that."

She paused, she wanted to say something else, and realised she had never said it to him before. "Thanks, George."

At this point she realised she had not thanked her daughter for helping tonight either. She turned and watched her getting the chicken out of the oven, tip the drained potatoes into the dish and baste them with the juices. She wanted to feel kindly towards her, but there had been so much animosity between them for so long, she felt mistrustful and just wanted to know what she was up to. Mrs Sarandon was not going to give in that easily.

"Thanks, Susan," she said, almost too quiet for her daughter to hear.

As she turned away she realised that the kitchen was not big enough for all three of them to cook in at once. She was facing the door, and her children were both busy. She went and stood in the entrance and leaned on the doorpost. She felt as though she could smoke a cigarette and just watch them. It was unusual now for her to think about smoking, she just leaned on the doorframe and watched them. She tried to imagine she had a cigarette, and tried to calm herself in the same way that having one would have done, she stayed still, breathed deeply, and just watched.

The meal was nearly done, except they had to wait. The vegetables had to finish off, and they had to make the gravy, but that was it. Much to her relief neither of her children asked why she was cooking a roast; she really did not feel like explaining the whole magazine thing.

They were just about getting to the point of standing around with nothing to do, when Adam came in with a bottle of wine.

"You're all in here . . . I'm sat out there in the sitting room, in a comfortable chair, on my own. I can hear you, you know, all here having a good time and ignoring me."

He was grinning as he spoke.

"I know all good parties end up in the kitchen, so I thought I'd join you in here. If you're all trying to avoid me it's tough."

He had opened the wine, and squeezed into the kitchen past his wife to get some glasses out of the top cupboard. They did not drink wine very often in this house, and the wine glasses had ended up being kept out of the way.

"Adam, what are you doing?" Mrs Sarandon was smiling, she did not mind having wine, but it was not a special occasion, and it was mid-week too.

"Well," he looked straight at her and seemed slightly sad as he said, "No one's arguing and everyone's in the same room, honey, it seems like a reason to celebrate to me."

As he turned round she could see he had only got three glasses down.

Susan was the first to react, and she did it immediately. She rolled her eyes and the noise she made was a sharp, contemptuous hissing breath out, through her teeth. Her Mum saw Susan's reaction at the same time as she saw the three glasses. At first she assumed Susan was annoyed that she was being left out, that Adam was being a little strict about Susan not being eighteen yet, and that she would somehow get blamed by Susan for this. She leapt to Adam's defence, saying,

"It's a school night, dear, what did you think, we were going to let you drink on a school night?"

It was not until she saw her husband redden and fumble around that it dawned on her it had been George he had left out.

Adam was acutely embarrassed at having got three glasses, what had he been thinking? He was not sure whether to admit that she was mistaken, that he had got a glass for their daughter, just not for her son, or whether to let it go and risk Susan being annoyed with him. He tried to reach back up for a fourth glass and make it look as though he had intended to get four all along. The fact that he had closed the cupboard made it obvious he had not . . . he did not really think anyone was fooled. He carried on though, he did what he had always done when he made mistakes. He stayed quiet and denied it . . . pretended it never happened, and waited for it to move on and be forgotten.

Adam carefully poured four equal glasses of wine and handed them round. They all raised their glasses, and looked towards him for the toast . . . this had been his idea, what should he say now?

"To us, to our family, and to an evening free from fighting."

They all mumbled a repeat of his last phrase and drunk together. The silence that followed was an expectant one which Mrs Sarandon eventually broke.

"How's those veg coming on then?"

George looked at his watch.

"Another three and a half minutes, Mum, and they'll be done."

Everyone was surprised to hear George answer.

Adam raised his glass again in surprise, "I'll drink to that! Whatcha doin' George? You cookin' us our suppa?" He took another deep gulp of his wine and smiled uncomfortably at no one in particular. Adam always talked to George like this, it annoyed everyone, even Adam himself felt uncomfortable about it, but he did not seem to be able to talk normally to George any more.

"Yes, I'm a good cook, Dad, I do this at College."

"Well, yes, dear," his Mum jumped in and tried to explain, "Actually both kids have been helping tonight. We're having chicken, a proper roast. It's taken a bit longer than I had thought, sorry, dear, but it's nice that you came in and joined us. The wine is lovely, thank you."

The light from the kitchen reflected on her glasses and he could not see his wife's eyes as she moved over and kissed him. He put his arm round her and grinned at Susan, who rolled her eyes.

The evening was starting to take on the feel they all got when people came to visit. A kind of pretend family acting, a veneer of politeness and shallow niceties, which Susan hated. It made her more uncomfortable when they all pretended to get along than it did when they were being horrible to each other.

"OK," George was holding up his arm showing his watch around the room, "It's all done now, you know?"

Susan was shocked that he could do that. He may not be able to read, but he must have known how long they needed and so worked out what time they would be done. She thought it was a good idea for George to show what he could do before he told them he wanted to leave home. She had been trying to help him as much as she could.

The tension dissolved into action and they all got on in the tiny kitchen to finish the food off, and get everything ready to sit down to finally eat it. Adam took plates and cutlery through and pulled out the folding table in the front room. There seemed to be an unvoiced decision to sit properly and eat together, not have plates on their laps in front of the TV news as usual. The news had finished anyway, so Adam laid the table properly, and poured more wine. Susan drained the carrots, her Mum saw to the chicken and potatoes, which left George calmly and quietly in the corner of the kitchen making gravy.

The meal began well enough, everyone was smiling, rosy cheeked from the heat in the kitchen and the wine on empty stomachs. They were hungry and looking forward to the food.

"Hey, Susan, you know, I had a dream about your computer game upstairs just now. I lay down, you know, tired, and I was in the game, you know, huge big cavern," George waved a fork in an arc above his head as he spoke, "And there was this really really bright light, you know, angel . . . "

Susan's heart thumped and she sat frozen, with a piece of chicken halfway to her mouth, half chewed peas visible in her open mouth, staring at George. She was transfixed, from the moment he said there had been a bright white light above him in *her* caves from *her* game, right through George telling the whole dream, she did not move a muscle. As he talked her own dream came flooding back to her, forgotten until that moment. She listened to someone else tell her own dream to her. She went cold, and one thought crashed and rolled through her mind.

When he finally finished, the piece of chicken slowly made its way back to her plate. Susan did not take her eyes off him. She swallowed her mouthful and leaned forward.

"George, I'm going to ask you something now and I want you to tell me the truth. I'm not going to be mad at you, I promise, but you have to tell me. Have you been sneaking into my room and playing my game while I'm out?"

"Oh no! George! You wouldn't have! George, you know not to go . . . "

"Now, George, you know you must never go . . . "

George held his sister's gaze and nodded to her under the sudden noise from their parents. They saw him nodding as they both said the word 'go' and they fell silent simultaneously.

Susan just sat, it all made sense now! The way Oemor had been frightened and disorientated whenever she started the game, the feeling of relief, seemingly when he realised where he was. Susan had accepted that she could feel his emotions as well as him feeling hers. Whether it was supposed to happen or not . . . she could not find anything in the stuff she read about which said anything about it . . . it had become clear to her that suddenly having stray and odd emotions while playing really was her feeling his reactions as he played.

She sat in the silence, her mind racing, her eyes moving erratically as she followed the thoughts in her head. If George had been playing and had not figured out how to save the game, that would mean . . . her heart sank at the thought of it, Oemor was falling down that open shaft at the top every time George had played the game. No wonder the poor guy was terrified every time she started him off, and the relief must be that he was not falling! That made sense to her now. What did not make any sense to her and was sending shivers of dread and excitement through her was that George had had her dream.

How could that be possible? It must be a part of the game . . . it had to be, but how? Susan was bordering on being frightened; she became aware of herself sitting immobile at the table, still staring at George who was now hanging his head in that stupid 'bad puppy' way he did to get himself off the hook. She focused herself, came to, and spoke to him gently,

"Come on, George, don't pull that cute sympathy look on me, you know it won't work. I'm not going to be mad at you, I said I wouldn't. I mean, in principle, I'm furious of course . . . Mum and Dad are right, you should never, ever, go into my room without me being there, OK?"

George nodded, still hanging his head.

"But I'm not bothered about that right now, what I'm bothered about is this spooky game I'm playing. Mum . . . "

Susan looked round to her mother, who was silenced and amazed by her daughter's calm response to this astonishing violation of her privacy. For once she would have been on Susan's side if she had flown off the handle at George, which would have been much more in character. Something very strange was clearly happening with both children this evening, and as Susan turned to her she clutched her wine glass to her chest for reassurance.

Susan spoke quickly, leaning forward over her dinner with an odd panic in her eyes.

"I need to buy something new for the computer, Mum, it's like a head piece, it's new, but it will mean I can talk to Oemor, I need to talk to him, Mum. George has frightened him. You don't know how to save a game do you, George? Or start a saved one?"

George's face was blank with wide-eyed incomprehension.

"No, I didn't think so. So, Mum, he's been really frightened lately and I couldn't figure out why, and now I know: it's George making him fall every time. I've got to tell him, I need to reassure him . . . and let him know it won't happen again."

As she spoke her body swooped round from the shoulders as her attention switched between the two of them. She was leaning forward, almost out of her seat. Her plate had been pushed forward and was half off the placemat, with gravy about to spill onto the wooden table surface.

"Well . . . " her mother took a breath. So, she had been right, Susan did want something.

" . . . you're not making any sense, Susan, but you're clearly asking for some money to buy something, so why don't you just tell us how much it costs and we'll see what we think."

"It's £79.99 Mum, but I've got to get one, especially now George has scared him, Mum. Please!"

"You've got to be kidding!" Adam broke in, his voice harsh and loud. "Eighty quid? For more computer stuff? When we saved up and worked extra shifts to get you the bloody thing in the first place? No Way!"

He put his glass down carefully and pointed to the ceiling where Susan's bedroom was.

"That computer, young lady, is to help you with your school work. You know . . . your classes? That place of learning we send you off to every day? If I ever saw you getting on and learning anything from that school, if you ever came to me and said 'Dad, I need eighty quid for my school, for my studies,' I'd give it to you, Susan, do you understand? If you ever showed us any hint that you appreciate what we have done for you to get you a good education, you could have the money, whether I could afford it or not. But for a bloody game?"

"Adam, dear, we said no shouting at each other tonight."

Adam did not miss a beat at this interruption, but his voice, which was getting increasingly loud, now lowered. His anger was palpable and seemed worse when he spoke quietly.

"You want us to spend even more money so you can waste your life not learning anything? No way, Susan, no way. You don't deserve anything like that, not till I see you getting on at school, no."

Adam sat back, started to fold his arms but seemed to change his mind and reached for his wine glass instead, drank all of it, and poured himself some more. As he poured he held up a finger to everyone to indicate he had more to say, he took another sip and carried on.

"You just don't get that we're really poor do you, Susan? Eighty quid? That's nearly a week's wages for your Mum. Since we moved house . . . which we did, by the way, for you to get a better education and get you away from that bad crowd of kids . . . we have no money, Susan, none. Certainly not if you want a holiday this year, you two. No Way. Not eighty quid, we ain't got it, and we wouldn't give it to you for a game even if we did."

He sat back, his voice trailing off; he looked at his wine and cradled the glass in both hands, shaking his head.

"You made us move so that I would leave all my friends behind . . . you made me go to a school where no one likes me . . . deliberately? Are you serious? You moved because of *me*?" Susan asked.

"Yes . . . " her mother answered, "Yes we did. We didn't know you wouldn't make new friends, you made such a good job of it the first time. You've never had trouble making friends. We didn't move so that no one would like you . . . what kind of parents would that make us? No, of course not, we moved so you could go to a better school. And, yes, we thought that if you went to a school away from the kids who skipped classes you might at least turn up, even if you're still determined not to learn anything."

Now that it was out, and they were back to the usual style of argument, Mrs Sarandon was on a roll. The wine was making her feel warm and flushed, and she was saying more than usual.

"Why must you always see the worst in us, Susan? We want so much for you, and you do so little. You're intelligent, you're clever, and if you put your mind to it I'm sure you'd enjoy school and all it has to offer. I've never understood you, Susan, I always loved school."

"Yeh, Mum, but I'm not the loser you were."

"So much for no fighting," Adam said quietly to himself as he drank more of his wine.

"Anyway," said Susan, "I don't see why you should be picking on me this evening."

Susan was upset, the evening had lost all the pleasantness of earlier. They had said no, she felt like crying and the only way to stop herself was to do something. Something cruel and vindictive, something to justify not getting the money, a real reason for them to shout.

Adam almost laughed,

"Because you asked us for eighty pounds, that's why - we're not picking on you. You asked, we said no way, and now you're sulking."

Her mind was in turmoil, they had moved because of her? It had never occurred to her that they had any other reason for moving, other than Dad's promotion. She was furious with them, with this stupid meal, with the two of them for making it all happen like this. She wanted them to stop picking on her, stop saying it was all her fault. She wanted them to leave her alone.

She glared at George.

"Well, at least *I'm* not planning to leave home and shack up with my boyfriend."

She turned to her Mum, shoved the chair out from underneath her and as she walked out, she said the cruellest thing of all.

" . . . And at least I'm not going to be pregnant at seventeen either."

Susan's Mum felt her daughter's words stab accusingly at her, and somewhere inside she knew that Susan was right. She had got pregnant at seventeen, and her daughter was right to judge herself against that. Come to think of it though, she was not aware that Susan even had a boyfriend, so why would she say . . . and the second stab of awful dread and realisation swept over her as she looked to see the expression on her son's face.

George was flushed, looking uncomfortable, almost panicked. He had slightly risen in his chair, also perhaps wanting to leave the room after Susan.

"You, George?" she said "You're . . . what George? You're planning to . . . to what? Why did Susan say that, like that? Is that about you?"

"Well . . . " George paused and sitting back down he started again.

"Mum . . . Tracy and I . . . "

"Oh dear God, there's a woman! George, what did she do to you?"

Her first thought was that he had been molested, somehow, or manipulated. Some woman was taking advantage of him, using him somehow.

She turned, bewildered, to Adam.

"What's she done to him? What does she want?" and turning back to look at George, she leaned forward and grabbed his hand.

"Whatever she's doing to you, George, she will stop. You're not going anywhere, don't you worry, now you tell me, what's going on?"

"But, Mum, it's not like that. Tracy and I . . . she's my girlfriend you know? I love her, Mum, and we want to live together, you know? We want to be with each other in a nice quiet house . . . and cook together . . . and not shout. Mum, I love her . . . "

This he said with a tremor in his voice and a piercing look straight into her eyes. She had not seen George look like this before. He had said "I love you Mum," many times, it made her heart sing to hear it, but she had never heard him say that he loved anyone else, and she had never seen him look so determined, like he did now. She let go of his hand and sat back, staring at him.

"Did you know about this?" She was asking Adam, but did not take her eyes off George while she spoke.

"'Course not!" Adam looked up "How would I know? So . . . you've been duped by a beautiful woman have you?" He looked towards his wife as he said,

"You wanna be careful of beautiful women, Georgy-boy, they promise you the world and then they take it from you. You're growing up there, kid. You're a man now, and women have power over men, they make us do all kinds of things. It's a kind of blind madness, George, love is. Don't let her seduce you, whatever she's

74

doing to you, you take care of yourself, look out for number one, George." He patted George on the chest as he said 'number one', but his eyes had remained firmly locked on to his wife's while he spoke.

There was a heartbeat of silence in the room, and then his mother said,

"I want to meet her."

Chapter 6

After their meeting with Tim, Tracy was not sure what to say for the best. How much should she tell Tim now?

She told her Mum last week, who had just ignored her. She had also told her Dad the next day and he had hit her. Hard. He had called her a "Fucking retarded whore" and threatened to kill George if he ever went near her. She had not been surprised that this had been his reaction. He was drunk when he arrived, and this is what happened when he turned up drunk.

No. The truth was not going to help anyone here, let alone her and George. Anyway, she never wanted George to know about Dad. She decided she would have to tell Tim something that sounded believable, but did not commit her to any lie she could be found out on. She could not say her parents were dead, she had tried that once before so she knew they would check.

She did know her Mum had her money, she had seen the book with her name on in the drawer next to the sink. She understood what Tim said about the money being hers, but she also knew that money was what kept Mum in cigarettes, gin and got some of their food each week. She had never said anything because she could see it was important. They did not seem to have any other money apart from when Dad dropped by and waved new notes around and they all got drunk. Thinking about it there must be more, because Mum went out to work every day, and now for the first time Tracy guessed that the money her Mum got from work must pay for the house.

Tracy's mind raced, fashioning a palatable truth for Tim.

*   *   *

Oemor was running before he knew where he was, he ran fast and straight at the next wave of Nephillim. He could hear them approaching, and prepared his gun and tried to get a grip on his emotions. He was awash with fury and upset anger, reckless in his approach; he started shooting before he could see anything. He shot wildly, blindly at nothing at all, venting anger and ammunition at empty rock walls. He ran and fired, killed many giants until there were no more bullets, then he did the most extraordinary thing, he stood and cried. He couldn't help it, he felt helpless to stop the rush of tears. He just wept, and as a Nephillim ran openly towards him he remained immobile. He saw the jaws opening above his head, looked into the open mouth with horror and screamed through his tears the one name that had any meaning,

"SUSAN!"

Oemor was running before he knew where he was, he ran fast and straight at the next wave of Nephillim. He was awash with fury and upset anger, reckless in his approach; he started shooting before he could see anything. Not again! He felt sadness and fury, he shot more deliberately, but he was exactly where he had just been, doing exactly what he had just done.

The bullets ran out exactly as they just had and the Nephillim approached, he saw the same thing happen, the mouth opening wide above him, the wave of sickening horror, he was disorientated, and was not thinking about the woman he loved at all. His mind was full of memory, this had only just happened. He fought the words as they rose in his throat, and as he saw the flesh-strewn teeth lowering over his head, he was driven to cry out. He managed to scream the only word that had any meaning,

"NO!"

Oemor was running before he knew where he was, he ran fast and straight at the next wave of Nephillim. What was going on? He was awash with confusion and upset anger, reckless in his approach; he started shooting before he could see anything. Oemor did not understand. He knew that he came back where he had left off, or back at the beginning falling down the shaft. He knew that events repeated themselves, and that whenever he died he had a chance to do it again, to learn from his mistakes and survive so he could go on. But this was different, somehow he was coming back and repeating his mistake, feeling anger and sadness he had never known.

Susan felt a wave of confusion. She had heard him shout 'No' instead of her name, and she realised that she was feeling Oemor's feelings. It was not fair for her to just use the game to vent her anger, she was making him die, making him come back and die again, just because she felt so bad. She turned the game off and threw herself on the bed. It was not fair! She could not even use her game to escape from the meal and the turmoil of feelings from it.

She had left, just walked out. This was not unusual, but she really wanted to know what was happening to George. She needed to know what it all meant for her too.

She could not think straight, she could barely think at all. Tears fell uncontrollably, her throat ached, her nose was running, she hated everyone, and she hated feeling like this. She hated having a stupid game that was so good she could not even use it to be angry and just shoot things. Oemor's feelings were so strong, she could not do that to him. She lay on top of the covers, occasionally crying, occasionally reddening with anger, gazing at the wall, and tried to go beyond the emotions that overwhelmed her. She tried to just calm down.

As she started to relax she thought back to the beginning of the meal, and her stomach flipped as she remembered George's dream. He had had the exact same dream as her, right down to the angel saying the same thing to him. Also, as she thought about it now, what he had found in the rock face sounded like it could only be the c-cylinder she had used to break the initial fall.

A sickening, awe-struck shiver ran coldly down her back as the thought occurred to her that the dream was sending messages about the game to the players. Telling George to use the c-cylinder so Oemor did not have to keep falling? It was impossible, ridiculous. The game telling her that George had been playing by showing her his hand and his severed head? She needed to get up and move about to get rid of the thought. Pacing up and down in her room felt silly, it was too small for more than two steps each way. She sat in front of the computer screen in a state of disbelief and horror. What was going on? She had forgotten all about her own dream until she heard George tell his, and this message had been the strongest consistent factor – they had both been told to shoot for the feet. The only thing she could think to do was try out what the angel had said, and see what happened. It was so weird, she started to smile at herself as she went back into the same saved game.

Oemor was back, same place, same situation but feeling completely different. He was calm, sad and curious. He was soon facing the same group of Nephillim he had just killed and been killed by three times. He tried to raise his gun to fire at them, but found that he could not; he was aiming at the floor!

What on earth was going on now?

He had broken free from this kind of trap before and he knew he could do it again. When he had gone back for the gun right at the beginning recently he had learned how to force his body to move through where it was being pushed. Oemor fixed his mind's energy on moving his arms upwards, raising the gun so he could shoot the giants who were now descending on him with alarming speed.

He managed it. Turning his whole body back to get the gun had been harder than raising his arms was now, moving his arms through his arms, feeling the stretch from where they were to where he needed them to be, he shot the Nephillim in the face, as he always had, and they shrieked and disappeared as they always did.

All his strength and power went in to keeping the gun up, to defending himself and staying alive this time. Finally the wave of ravaging enemies was gone, he had made it and he was still alive, though he was scratched and had some deep gashes. He used up the last of his first aid to fix these. He was low on ammo and had run out of food, but he was safe for the moment, and he had survived to face the next onslaught. Oemor felt strong and pleased with himself.

Susan stopped playing and saved the game, she let go of the joystick and sat immobile staring at the screen. What was that all about? She had decided to shoot at their feet, like the angel had said, but had been unable to. The game had not let her shoot at the feet at all; she had ended up shooting them in the face, no matter what she did.

She thought it could not be programming, as she had previously been able to shoot the gun wherever she had wanted to; there was a massive amount of control aiming and even how to carry the gun, it had been one of the features she had liked about the game – she had been able to shoot at anything, in any way.

The feelings from the joystick had been of determined battle, but that was surely because she had been fighting five of the giants at once, which was more than she had before. She turned away from the screen, got up, and started to pace up and down again. It felt better to be moving than sitting still, so she stepped and turned, stepped and turned while trying to think about the game and the programming. It was a learning program. That meant that the situations it encountered, it remembered and then applied the knowledge of what had worked to the next similar situation. Oemor must have 'learned' that shooting giants in the face killed them, therefore that is what he would do whenever he encountered a giant.

She also realised that this was the same saved game where she had just deliberately killed him twice. Susan stopped walking and stood still as she really thought for the first time that Oemor might remember saved games; even though he returned to the same place, he might remember what had happened to him.

That was so strange, but it made some sense. Lately it had started to feel as though the computer was moving before she was, and once or twice he had ducked, or taken a turning before she had moved her hand. She had just thought that she must have done it without realising it, but was it possible for Oemor to be moving by himself? Susan did not think that it was possible but then what was the point in having a program that could learn otherwise.

As she thought things through, carefully and methodically, she realised that, without the *Nephillim Caves* master com, the only way she could possibly communicate with Oemor was through the gaming journal. What would be the point of writing, if it was not part of the program? It was the only thing she could think to try, and it was a long-shot. Could they possibly have programmed in a way of interpreting written text into the Oemor program? Probably not, but it was worth a try. What else was she going to do?

She remembered that she had written a little bit about the dream before, but not what the angel had said. This time she would have to make it clear that she believed the dream was a message, and that she wanted him to try doing what it had said. She decided to write in the journal that she had had the dream again, and say exactly what the angel said, and what she thought he should do. Susan did not like to think too much about the fact that she was clearly making something up for her computer in order to try and trick it into letting her do something it had stopped her from doing. Was she going mad? Was she really going to do this? She chuckled to herself, shook her head wistfully and sat down to type her first lie in the journal.

Chapter 7

Adam had nursed his sore head for a week after That Damn Meal. First of all he had a hangover, but then he just kept playing it over and over again in his mind – everything he had said to Susan, the way he had behaved. Their Mum had been right, it was him who had toasted a night of no raised voices, and then he had been the first to break his own toast. And the things he had said to Susan, terrible things for any daughter to have to hear. Fancy her knowing that they just moved to take her away from all her friends. It was a terrible thing to have done. They had not meant it like that, he knew that, but still, that must be how it seemed to her now after what he had said.

For Adam the worst of it was the way he had not got a glass for George. Even he did not really understand what had happened then. He could not remember it without moaning, and he could not help remembering it.

In the first love-drenched year of the new relationship, he had believed that he could fix George, somehow. He looked back now and felt so stupidly deluded by the whole thing; at the time he had thought perhaps he had just not been taught in the right way, not loved enough, not had a man around to help. Adam had believed something would be different, would change, and George would be all right.

He tried everything he knew, which did not seem like much now but at the time had truly been everything. He had spent a lot of time sitting with George working through the simplest maths he could think of, trying to get him to work out money, even some reading lessons he vaguely remembered from his own patchy education. None of it had made any difference. Nothing that Adam did changed George. The only thing that was different by the time Adam finally gave in and stopped was that George was calling him Dad instead of just Adam. Thinking about this now he thought it was the best thing that could happen, but at the time he had barely noticed. They had moved in by then, expecting their new baby, he was less in love and working all the hours he could to get everything they needed for the new child. He gave up on George just before Susan arrived, he had stopped everything he had been doing, and since then had very little to do with him.

George had learned eventually to stop coming to him with new questions, Adam never asked George anything else, and that was that. Adam had his wife and child to fill himself up with, there was little room for someone who did not respond to him properly.

*   *   *

"Wow. I feel so nervous, George!" Tracy held her boyfriend's hand and as they approached his front door she pulled him back, holding him to her in the street.

"Does she hate me do you think? Will she shout at me too?"

He took her face in his hands.

"How could she hate you? You're beautiful. I don't think she'll shout when you're here, she doesn't do that when other people are visiting, you know?"

Tracy knew what he meant. No one in her family shouted when they had people round either.

"OK then, let's go for it!"

They stepped up to the front door, and went in.

"We're here!" George called as they went through the door, but he did not have to. His Mum had been on the look out for the last twenty minutes, she had seen them up the street, she had watched them holding hands all the way to the house, stopping outside, looking unsure.

So she knew before she met Tracy that she was another one.

George's Mum had not been expecting this at all. In her own mind she had thought Tracy must have been some young care-assistant, or College tutor, or someone normal who was taking her George for a ride. In all of her imaginings about this woman she had somehow failed to imagine that she would be another Downs. Why had this not occurred to her? It was so obvious now she saw them together.

George's Mum realised, as she had come to the door, that if this were anyone else's son she would have smiled because they actually looked sweet together. They were the same size and body shape, they had almost the same face, except Tracy had blond hair and stood a half inch shorter than George. She looked up at him, and if he had been anyone else's son, George's Mum could almost have felt proud of him, how he had taken her face in his hands, brushed her hair from her eyes, and said words of reassurance which had caused them to face the door together. George's Mum knew that the door they were facing was her, and she felt dizzy and sickened at the whole idea of these two being together. In that first shock of realisation she hated Tracy so much more than she could have done if Tracy had been normal.

"Hello."

George's Mum pulled herself up to her full height and looked down at the disabled woman coming through her front door.

"You must be Tracy. George hasn't told us much about you." She refused to smile and shook the woman's hand as firmly as she could. "It's interesting for me to finally meet you, would you like to come in? I'll make some tea and we'll have a chat. The kettle's just boiled."

George's Mum almost ran to the kitchen as George showed Tracy through to sit in the front room. They went in and sat silently in the separate chairs rather than the sofa, which she was relieved about. At least she would not have to see them touching each other again. Not that, not yet.

She used the time making the tea to calm down and get over her shock. She knew she had to try and make this all right. She had seen over the last few days how important this was to George. She had felt more protective of him this week than she had since he was born. She had seen him getting nervous about this visit, about her judgement. She knew she should not go in to the room while feeling as angry as she did. She had seen over the last few days that whatever she might think, his emotions were real to him. She could see that George truly believed himself to be in love with this woman, and that if she got angry, he would be very hurt and upset. Until today she had thought to take this young woman to one side and give her a piece of her mind in private . . . tell her to back off and leave

George alone, but now she had seen her, she could not do that.

As the kettle clicked off she was already pouring the water onto the teabags and the steam rose swiftly and covered her glasses in a fog.

"Damn."

This always happened when she poured it too fast. She had to take them off; she could not see how full the kettle was. She stopped to take a breath and calm down. She was flustered by the whole thing and wished Adam could have been there. What was she going to do now? This girl probably thought she was in love with George as much as George thought he was in love with her! How could they have let this happen? Those people at the centre must have known about this; they should have stopped it.

"God, what a mess!" She knew they could not hear her, and saying it out loud helped her calm down.

She made the tea, put the pot on the tray and carried it all through. Not thinking where to start or what she was going to say, George's Mum blurted out the thought that was in her head while she walked through the door.

"So, Tracy, what does your Mum and Dad make of all this then?"

"My Mum is all right, she doesn't mind about George, but my Dad . . . "

There was a hesitation in her voice, not like George's long bewildered pauses, more deliberate, until she eventually continued,

"Well, my Dad was not too happy about it really."

"No, I bet he's not. And you might as well know right now neither am I. Not happy at all!"

Georges' Mum tried to stare Tracy down, but Tracy held her gaze until she had to look down to pour the tea. She could see that Tracy was not going to be easy to intimidate. She had been brought up to be a good hostess to visitors, and so she poured tea, passed a plate of biscuits and talked about the cold weather for a couple of sentences. It had been unfair to come in and ask that right off, she should at least be polite. Tracy sat back and started to relax, while George perched on the edge of his seat, sitting on his hands, as usual.

He looked up suddenly.

"Tim said he could meet you."

"Well who the hell is Tim when he's at home? How many people have you told about this, George, before you came and told your Dad and me?"

"Just Tim, Mum, he said he wants to help us."

"OK, fine, bring him along, why not. But I tell you, you're not going anywhere, George. You're staying right here, with me, in this house, where you belong. I'm your mother, George, I've got to look after you, and the best place for me to do that is for you to live here."

They looked at each other across the room, and it was a look that broke her heart. She could not let them see that.

"Now then, Tracy, I don't mean to be rude to you or anything, but this moving George out of his own home and away from his family, it just can't happen. I mean you can see that can't you? It's just not going to work . . . I mean, look at you, the two of you, you're not doing any such thing."

"You mean look at us because we're disabled don't you, Mrs Sarandon." Tracy was looking straight at her and Mrs Sarandon felt herself redden, shocked and embarrassed by Tracy's words. She had never properly talked to George about being disabled, or about being Downs Syndrome. She had told him he was special, and that there were some things he could not do, but clearly Tracy and this new person, Tim, had been talking to him about being disabled. His Mum had never liked to use the word. There was so much that George could not do, she wanted him to think about all the things he could do, not the things he couldn't. Obviously he was different from other people, but she had always been uncomfortable about telling him he was disabled.

She would have to meet this Tim person, who had been poisoning George's mind, and letting him believe he could do impossible things.

Then a sickening thought occurred to her . . . what if Tim was disabled too? What if it was just a whole group of them from the centre making up some kind of fairy-tale romance to talk about? She almost felt relief at the thought, if that was all this was, just them dreaming about a life they could never have, she would not have anything to worry about. She would just have to go and talk to the staff and tell them they had to put a stop to it. Explain to them it was cruel to let people like this think they could do things like move out, own houses and live together.

What if Tim was a member of staff after all? She would just have to explain it to him, it really did seem to be cruel to her, and the sooner she put a stop to all it the better.

"Well, OK, I'll meet this Tim person of yours then. OK, yes . . . all right, I will." She nodded and got up. Her tea was finished, she did not think she could cope with much more of this visit.

"George, do you want to show Tracy around the house before she goes? You should let her see where you live now, George, how nice it is here in our new house. You never bring friends back to play any more."

She said it to get them out, so she could breathe and think without the two of them staring at her in that intense, examining way. It was not until they had left the room and she heard them run, giggling up the two flights of stairs that she realised what she had done. She had practically sent those two off to a bedroom together! And, worse, she had said something about playing together! Well, she could not go straight up now it would be too rude. She would have to wait. Mrs Sarandon crept up the first flight of stairs and paced up and down on the landing, listening to her son upstairs with his girlfriend, trying to hear what they were doing. She thought that if she heard the bedsprings she would go straight up . . . that would be just too much. They seemed to be just talking. His Mum felt guilty and awkward hanging around underneath them, but she did not know what else to do. She could not just go downstairs and clear up, goodness only knew what they would get up to. She realised that this was all just too much for her. What was she doing? Hiding on the landing as though he was a teenager and this was his first girlfriend.

George had taken Tracy straight up to lie on his bed and look at the clouds. He had lain here so many times and thought of her, he wanted, just once, to lie and show her the sky from his room. They lay straight down and then heard his Mum following them up the stairs. They lay still and listened to her walk up and down the landing below them. George showed Tracy the clouds, the way they drifted slowly passed and changed shape, the pink hue as the sun set out of sight, how the blue got darker as it got later. They did not say much. Tracy had listened to George talking about the clouds before, and she knew his Mum was listening. She just wanted to lie close to him and see what he saw when she was not there. He stroked her hair and they lay for a long while watching the daylight leave and the night begin. Single stars appeared in the changing colour of the sky.

"Mum will be getting tired, you know? She's walked about a mile down there." They giggled quietly, and got up. He held her face in his hands again and kissed her once on the cheek before taking her hand and leading her downstairs. He touched her with such gentle tenderness Tracy felt more loved in that moment than if he had kissed her the whole time they were in his room. She loved him too, and as the dusk cast strange shadows across the unfamiliar surroundings, she was grateful to him for his guiding touch as he led her down the stairs.

"Well, you two took your time I must say." She was downstairs in the kitchen by the time they got there. Tracy thought she must have run to get there before them.

"Isn't it a lovely room, Tracy?"

"Yes, I like it," said Tracy, she was on her best behaviour still and so did not say she thought the view of the stars from his bed was very romantic. Any other circumstances she would have done, just to be provocative, but this was George's Mum, and it was better not to make her angry on their first meeting.

*   *   *

It had worked! He could not believe it! He must be in love with a true prophet, touched by the Gods! Something amazing was happening and Oemor was floating in a state of wonder, that he should be able to be a part of these magnificent events.

The woman he loved had dreamed a way for him to succeed against his enemies!

The bond between them was so strong that he knew her thoughts and had been able to do what her dream had said. This was amazing and the love he felt for her surpassed itself in strength and passion. Once they were free, there would be stories written about this! Ballads would be sung for years to come that told the tale of Susan and Oemor and the love strong enough to kill giants!

His heart was singing as he marched. This time, for the first time, he had bullets to spare, and he had just killed more Nephillim than ever before. He had done as the angel in Susan's dream had foreseen, he had shot at their feet, and they were gone, exploded into thin air with just one bullet.

As he turned a corner and entered a cavern, Nephillim swarmed at him from all angles. It looked as though they had some kind of dwelling here and he had just stumbled in and disturbed them. He backed up against the rock, kept his gun low, and aimed accurately and mercilessly for their feet. He watched the giants approaching, running into those he had already shot, saw them also disappear in the explosion. The shrieking noise they made as they died echoed round the walls of the cavern repeating as they came towards him and died one after the other, wave upon wave.

When the cavern was deserted Oemor moved through their belongings and picked up whatever he could find that might be useful. Up until this point he had found only food, ammo and first aid, but here there were shining purple stones, and a set of keys.

He picked up everything he could find, and put it all in his bag, as he always did.

There was some food here but it looked different. Oemor found that although he could pick it up, he could not eat it. In fact, when he tried to eat some of the giant's food it made him sick. Oemor had never experienced anything like this and was fascinated by the feeling, and the sight of his stomach contents coming out in front of him. He thought about being killed by them, how they had always eaten him by the head first. He did not even know what it was he was doing, but he never tried eating the food of the Nephillim again.

Oemor sat and ate some of his own food, which made him feel better, and he thought again about Susan's dream, and how she had asked him to try doing what the angel had told her. He reached into his pocket and pulled out a wallet. Up until that moment he had not remembered it was there, but he opened it with a familiar flourish and looked at the photograph inside of Susan. He lifted the image up and stroked the upturned face with his finger for a moment. The longer he was in the caves, the more he felt he understood her. It was not as though he could talk with her, he just knew what her thoughts had been. He had known her thoughts for some time now . . . daydreaming about school, teachers and other students and a brother, who seemed to have something wrong with him. This was the first time he knew she had been thinking of him. She did seem to know a lot about him, Oemor was not sure how . . . she knew he had a gun, that he was fighting giants and coming to rescue her. She could easily guess that he would come for her, but how she knew the details he was not sure.

It struck him, if he knew her thoughts so intimately, perhaps the same link meant that she also knew his. She must know then that he loved her so very much, and thought about rescuing her constantly. She would know also how frightened he was, and that he had occasionally been back at the beginning, miles away from her and knowing nothing about her. He worried that she would think this would mean he did not love her. If she could truly read his thoughts as clearly as he knew hers then she would know that that could never happen.

Oemor felt happier with this realisation. He got up and looked round, deciding which direction to head in next. As with all the large caverns of this sort, there were a few small cave entrances leading off it. To this point Oemor had been heading consistently in the same direction, which was leading him downwards slightly and into the heart of this labyrinth of caves. He could not be certain of course that this would lead him to Susan, but he thought he could spend a lifetime lost in this place, so it was better just to head in a straight line. Also, as he carried on in this direction he knew more and more of Susan's thoughts. The few times he had started back falling down the open shaft he had not known any new thoughts at all.

It made sense to Oemor that he would know more of her thoughts and feel her stronger as he got closer to her, and weaker if he was further away. So he assumed that he was heading in the right direction.

As he picked up the last of the ammo and jewels he could find, the rock rumbled in the familiar way, which indicated more Nephillim were on their way. He thought he might as well stay here in the open than try running down any of the caves. He was not sure exactly which cave to head down at the moment, there were two quite close to each other, which seemed to be going in the right direction. Oemor braced himself against the side of the cavern, back firmly and safely with rock behind it, feet square and secure on the ground, and gun aimed towards their feet, wherever they came at him from. As he waited and the rock rumbled with their calling, he listened to the sound. It was higher pitched than usual and louder, with still no sign of them. With this much noise he would expect them to be on top of him by now.

Oemor was getting scared, and he fired a few shots off into mid-air, just to check they had not got this close without him seeing them. The sound changed immediately to a high-pitched whistle which created an echo around the cavern. The combined noises hurt his ears. Oemor was still unable to see anything, and he shot again into the air in front of him, raising his gun slightly. It was impossible to shoot for the feet of something he could not see, and his fighter's instincts raised the gun in front of his torso for self-protection. The screaming grew even louder, and the air directly in front of him shimmered. Whatever it was it was no Nephillim; he had not seen anything like this before. He shot again at the disturbance in the air in front of him, and gradually he saw what it was.

A horned head was thrown back and screamed to the cavern above, blood was seeping from a wounded chest. As the air shimmered a solid figure appeared and Oemor could see it was a red, winged lion, with horns, talons, sabre teeth and a lashing tail. The tip of the tail glistened and as it thrashed past him Oemor realised it was as sharp as a blade. A blade? Oemor felt a memory rise from his distant past; he had kept a blade, a very good combat knife, down the side of his boot.

In the shock of seeing this horror appear in front of him, Oemor had shot at the chest and at the face of this thing. A red light flashed in his head . . . he was low on ammo, he took final aim, shrugged and shot for the feet of the new creature. In the silence that followed so many things happened Oemor did not realise straight away that the screaming had stopped.

It, whatever it was, recoiled. The wings beat in a new direction and it moved further away. As it did so the lethal tip of the tail whipped forward and knocked the gun from his hands. Cuts appeared on his palms as the gun fell to the ground. Oemor leaned forward slightly and looked at his hands. This was all he needed, he pushed his body further down, reached inside the top of his boot and found what he was looking for. His knife was still there! He took it and held it out, cutting towards the tail tip he took a step forward. His knife found purchase in the flesh just above the tip of the tail, the blade fell to the ground.

The scream rose to the roof once more as the creature cried out in pain, and in its distraction Oemor once more reached inside his leather tunic to his belt. The c-cylinder! He had almost forgotten about it until he felt his hand go to it. He reached, grabbed it and shook in one smooth motion. An observer would have thought that he had magically produced an eight-foot pole from thin air. He handled the c-cylinder in an old and familiar way, and turning it above his head he advanced on the howling lion. He aimed a blow to the chest, but instead of knocking the creature back, his pole sank deep into the chest, and he had to pull hard to get it out again. He aimed once more, and this time made a clear hit towards its face. A direct hit to the eye would have done some damage to it, but the lion ducked its head before the attack, and the pole reverberated off one of the huge horns, a blow which knocked them both backwards.

Oemor was the first to recover, he regained his balance, held the pole in a fighting stance and waited. With talons extended and horns forward this winged beast was a foreboding new enemy, and Oemor did not know how to attack now. Despite the injuries he had inflicted on it, it was still flying steadily only a few feet away from him. It had made no direct attack on him. He was sure it would have won if it had, so Oemor just stood his ground. Slowly it flew a few inches closer, and when it was within reach it swiped a paw at his c-cylinder and knocked it clean from his hands.

This was it, Oemor knew he had no defence left now, and he had no clue how to defeat this thing. All he had left was a first aid kit and those jewels he had found from the Nephillim. In a forlorn last-ditch attempt he reached for the jewels and threw one of them. To his astonishment the lion caught the shining rock in its mighty paw, and placed the jewel inside its wounded chest.

Oemor watched in amazement, and tried it again. It did the same thing, swooping slightly lower and coming slightly closer to him. With its head high and waiting, talons retracted inside the massive paws, red wings beating steadily behind it, he somehow did not feel as though it was about to kill him. The creature actually looked straight at him, directly into his eyes, and Oemor felt a shiver of excitement as he threw another of the jewels for it. Again it caught it and placed the rock on one of its wounds. Oemor could see now that where the rocks had been placed, the wounds were healing over. He was astonished and threw more, one at a time, until he had only one left. The mighty winged lion at this point also had one wound left in the end of its tail, and Oemor thought he would try something different. He stepped forward and reached for the creature's tail, which hung limp and twitching a few inches from the ground. The creature moved away slightly, so he held up the rock so it could see that he had one and took another step towards it. It held its ground and he reached to pick up the tail. Oemor gently and accurately placed the purple jewel into the end of the tail where his own knife had severed it minutes earlier. On contact with the lion's blood the rock turned dull and grey as the others had, the bleeding stopped. Soon the tail was growing and glowed as it healed. A new blade did not grow back, but the tail was better, and Oemor was out of jewels. He wondered what would happen now.

*   *   *

George was disillusioned and upset. He felt bogged down with all the things that he and Tracy could not do. Their first flush of excitement seemed long gone, his Mum was not happy about any of it and Tracy was annoyed with everyone for not letting them get a house straight away. George was despondent. Whatever was going to happen to them, it was clearly going to drag on for a long time, and nothing would really change for them for ages.

Tim had arranged a visit for them to go and see Nicola and Andy, and he was trying to get George's Mum to go and see Nicola's Mum. George was not sure why she was not going to see Andy's Mum, but it seemed like a good idea anyway. Tracy was on her way round and they were going off to Nicola and Andy's together with Tim. That was one thing that had changed a lot; Tracy now came round to his house quite often. She had never been to his house before, but now that Mum had invited her round once, she came whenever she wanted. George really enjoyed her visits and it meant they were more relaxed when they were together at College and the day centre.

Her distinctive knock at the door sounded through the house and he got up and ran downstairs. Opening the door to her grinning face he could not help but feel lifted.

"Why don't you ever, you know, ring the bell? Everyone else does."

"Because everyone else does," she said as she kissed him. He did not understand, but did not care either, so he kissed her back and took her into the front room to wait for Tim.

"How are you feeling?" Tracy said.

"Nervous I think. I'm all, you know, stomach hurts like at sports day before your race. Dad said that was nervous."

"Yeh, me too a bit. I hope they're nice and tell us how they did it."

"Mmmmm," George nodded, looking down, "yeh, so we, you know, can get it."

"Well, we will get it, George, you know that we will."

"Oh, you know, I meant understand it, how they did it, so we can copy them. That's the point isn't it?"

The door bell rang, Tracy checked her watch as George got up to answer it.

"I'll say one thing for him, he's punctual that's for sure."

George opened the door to Tim.

"Hey guys, ready to roll? I'm badly parked."

"Yes, we're waiting now." He turned back and shouted into the house "Tracy, we're going straight away."

George got his coat and they left the house together. Following Tim down the steps the early morning sun shone through his ginger hair making a sun-lit glow around the top of his head. George found this strangely comforting; maybe Tim really was going to sort it all out for them.

Nicola and Andy were not Downs, and Tracy felt a slight shock of disappointment. Of course, she knew other people had learning disabilities, but still, when Tim had said they were like her and George she had assumed.

"Hello, Tim, are these them?"

Andy opened the door and glanced up at Tim as he spoke.

"Yup, we're all here, Andy, this is Tracy and this is George."

"Hi, come in. Take your shoes off please, it keeps the carpets clean. We're all going to sit in the sitting room, there is a sofa for you. Tim, you have your seat, I have mine and Nicola has said she will perch."

"Okey-dokey then, come on in you two, take your shoes off like he says and then come on through."

Tim was nervous too, Tracy realised. He must be, he was fussing. He had ushered them past Andy, so that despite the formal introduction she had not yet shaken his hand. This was all a bit odd. Andy talked like a lot of people she knew at the centre, and he had not yet looked at her or George. There was someone who was like this in her computer class and it had taken Tracy a long time to get to like him. She thought Andy would probably be like that too.

The house was a bit bigger than hers, and Tracy really liked the way it all looked new; the decoration and the furniture looked as though it had all been put in yesterday. She knew Andy and Nicola had been in their house for a few months now. It made her wonder how old her own house was. She decided she would have to talk with her Mum about how she got their house. They did not own it, she knew it was the council's house. That was what her and George were going to have. That was what this house was, and it was really posh.

Nicola came in to the front room as they were sitting down, she limped a little and held her left hand up at her waist all the time. Tracy looked at her face and almost gasped. She had been looking at the boots with metal supports at the top, so Nicola was already saying hi to Tim and turning towards her before she saw her face. She was, Tracy thought, the most beautiful woman she had ever seen. She had long dark hair, really white teeth, a huge wide smile and eyes that just lit up as she looked into them. Tracy thought Nicola could have been on the front of a magazine except for her arm and leg. She stood up and put her hand out.

"Hi, I'm Tracy, I'm very pleased to meet you. I love your house."

"Hi Tracy. Good to meet you too. Do sit and be comfortable, the kettle has boiled, what would you like to drink?"

As she took the orders for drinks and turned to go Tracy realised that everyone was gazing at Nicola. She really was beautiful, even Tim was watching the door as she left. George looked at her and flushed deeply, so she took his hand to show it was all right. Tracy knew George loved her, he had just been as surprised as her at the way Nicola looked.

"You want to know how we got the house then?" Andy said, "I have made a list, I think with everything in, of how we got the house. But it might not be the same for you."

"Yeh, great, Andy," Tim said "That would be really useful I mean, obviously everyone's situation is going to be different, but it would be a big help to get an idea of what happened for the two of you. A list would be perfect."

"Shall I get it now?"

"Well, yeh, you might as well while we all get drinks and settle down."

Andy rose and walked out of one door as Nicola came in from the kitchen with four coffees. She had a tray with a handle over the top so she could carry all the drinks by herself. That was neat. Tracy wondered how many other things Nicola had to make sure she could do ordinary stuff with only one hand.

Andy's list proved to be less helpful than she had hoped. They had applied for a council house, had social workers assess them, talked with Tim about what they wanted and then moved in when the house had been offered. A lot of the difficulties had been more practical than anything else.

"So," she asked, "What were your families like about it? Nicola, how was your family? Did they all think it was all right for the two of you to live together?"

"No. No, not at first," Nicola put her mug on the floor as she spoke, and her hair fell forward over her face. "My Mum was dead against it at first. She thought that, with only one hand that works, there was loads I couldn't do. And she couldn't get how great Andy is, not like I do. She was more frightened for me I think, but she got really angry about it all, isn't that right, Tim?"

"Yes, well, yeh, she was upset and frightened, much like your Mum, George. That's why I thought it would be useful for them to meet. If your Mum could talk with someone who shares her fear and concerns, but now it's happened and she's quite happy isn't she, Nicola, now?"

"Oh yeh, she's fine. She's not going to get on well with Andy, but I can live with that. I'm here and the two of us are together. That's the main thing."

This made Tracy smile. It was the kind of thing she would say about her and George. She also knew that George's Mum was probably never really going to accept her, but she could see that Nicola was right. It was not as important as her and George getting to be together.

The conversation went on, Andy said very little apart from what he read from his list. He did not look up the whole time. Tracy tried hard to remember it was probably part of his disability, not that he was being rude. After a while it started to irritate her anyway, it really felt rude even if he was not meaning it. Nicola and Tim went over the whole story of how they had got the house, and how they had dealt with the problems. Even though their problems were not the same as hers and George's, she started to really believe that some day she and George would be sitting in their house explaining how they had overcome their problems to another couple. Perhaps that was the way with problems, perhaps that was what Tim was for, he always saw a problem by how it could be solved. Maybe that was it, maybe they had to just solve everything, rather than getting depressed about how difficult it all was.

George lay on his bed, gazed at the sky, and wondered what he could do to feel more excited about everything they were trying to do. He had not found the trip to Nicola and Andy's as helpful as he had hoped. Their situation was very different to him and Tracy.

George was realising that he knew very little about Tracy's home, her Mum and Dad, and how they were reacting to all this. The attention was all on his Mum, not hers, just like they had only talked about Nicola's Mum, not Andy's.

He sighed and turned over, wanting to think of something else. He thought again about Susan and what she had said the day he first told her they were moving in together. This time he did not think about being disabled, he cast his mind back and replayed her exact words. She had said something else and he could not quite remember what. Then it came back to him, her voice, the earnest look on her face, she had said it would be like if they got married. He lay still and remembered how he had felt, and knew that he should ask Tracy to marry him.

That was it!

He sat up. If they were engaged to be married no one could argue that they should not live together. He wanted to do it right, he sat up and turned the light on. Because George could not read or write he had learned to rely on his mind much more to remember important things. He would leave clues for himself, and sometimes he organised his room in particular ways, to remember particular things. These arrangements had significance for him, he had learned to use patterns around him to help him remember, just like a note. This time he needed to remember that he was going to marry Tracy, and make a list of the things he would need.

He gazed around the room . . . what could he do? He needed a ring, to wear a suit and to get down on one knee in a romantic place.

None of this was going to be easy, but the more time he spent thinking about it, the more likely he was to remember it all. He got up and opened his wardrobe door. Looking right to the back he found the suit he had worn to his granddad's funeral a few years ago. He got it out and hung it on the outside of the door. Adam had cut a small notch in the top of the door so that George could hang clothes on the outside and still close the wardrobe; he hung his suit on that notch now, so he could see the suit from his bed. Over to the left he had a mirror and a shelf with hairbrush, comb, deodorant, shaver and aftershave. He moved to the shelf and took everything off. He wiped all the tiny bits of hair onto the floor so the shelf was clean and placed everything back on, but he placed them all so that they made a neat circle on the shelf.

Finally George got a single red sock out of his drawer, stood on his bed and fixed it to the window. He sat back down at the head of the bed and looked around his room. The suit was clear and he would see it every time he got clothes out. The ring was obvious now but he would have to remember to put everything back in the same place whenever he used them. The sock would be fine and made sense when combined with the other things . . . for George, looking up at something red whenever he looked out of his window would be enough for him to remember 'a romantic place'.

It was good, it would work and George smiled to himself. Now all he had to do was find that romantic place, get a ring, and borrow Adam's shirt and tie again. It seemed to be a more achievable goal than getting a house at the moment. George decided he would do it, he would do it all by himself and he would do it all in secret. The most obvious person to ask for help and the person he always wanted to help him out was Tracy herself, but not this time, this time George would have to do it alone.

He lay back down and his mind wandered to the character in Susan's computer game. Oemor was strong and brave and was fighting with giants just to save the woman he loved. George liked the romantic side of the story, a strong capable soldier who was so in love he was risking his life for his woman. Although George had not been able to play the game very well, he had felt the fear and excitement from the joystick, it had felt new and different. He wanted to be more like Oemor. To free Tracy from the cave she was chained in and take her away from giants and monsters. Yes, George wanted to be the man who would save Tracy, and the suit and a ring was what he needed to do it.

Everyone had been saying to him that George had no money, but that was not strictly true. He had been given pocket money when he was younger, and was still given money every now and then. There had been a few times when George had tried to spend his money, and the person who had taken him shopping had bought what he had wanted for him. Mum did it all the time, his

Dad did it too sometimes, and so did Aunty Jeanne, who took him out on a Saturday sometimes. He had heard Mum telling Aunty Jeanne that he could not go out on his own, so if she was going into town would she mind taking George. George knew that she went into town without him more often than she came to pick him up as he had seen her at the bus stop. He did not mind, he did not want to go every time she came and he had not worked out how to say no.

This meant that George did have some money in the wallet he kept in a drawer by his bed. He did not know how much it was, but there were some notes and some coins. He liked to have the coins because of the clinking noise they made when he walked with them in his pocket. He sounded like Dave from work walking down the corridor, and sounding like staff made him smile. All the trips into town with Aunty Jeanne meant George knew the bus journey very well. He had done it so many times, he knew where to get on, what to say to the driver, and when to stand up to get the bus to stop in the right place. George decided that he was going to go into town on his own, with his own money, and buy a ring for Tracy. He giggled at the thought of it until his nose snorted. He lay on the bed and smiled.

Chapter 8

Tracy was also feeling upset and disheartened with how moving in with George was going, because nothing was going at all. Her own mother still dismissed the idea so completely it was obvious she did not believe it at all. Her Mum had said,

"Alton Towers" and walked out the last time Tracy had mentioned it.

For Tracy and her Mum 'Alton Towers' had become a shorthand way of referring to something that you get excited about and then never happens. It was two years ago now, and neither of them had forgotten. The centre had said that they were organising a trip to Alton Towers. Tracy had brought the form home with high hope . . . she did not know what it was, but it sounded grand, almost like somewhere royal, and it would be something different, something to look forward to for the summer when College had finished. Her Mum had frowned, tutted and shaken her head, asked her three times if she *really* wanted to go to this place, did she know what it was like? Would she enjoy the rides? Tracy had said yes, and had become more emphatic the more her Mum had quizzed her. Finally, her Mum had signed the form, and said they would be living off beans for a month.

Tracy had no idea really what Alton Towers was and so had asked at the centre. John had laughed.

"You've signed the form, you're going, don't you think you should have found out beforehand what it is you're going to?"

"Whatever it is, it'll be better than being stuck here all day," she had said, straight back.

Tracy asked everyone in the Jigsaw group and although a few of them were going, not many of them knew exactly what it was. They said Edward had been, she should ask him. Edward was posh, and had done everything, so she asked him. When Edward told her he was not going because all there had been was roller-coaster rides he could not go on, there had been no towers at all, and he had had to sit in a teacup with seven-year-old kids because he was too short for the other rides her heart sank. She was shorter than Edward.

Still, it was going to be a day away from the centre, George was going and that was enough. He had also got his Mum to sign the form without knowing what it was about, and when she told him what Edward had said he had taken her hand and shrugged.

"If the sun shines it will be nice. We'll find a dry bit of grass and sit together."

They had only just started going out then, and she thought it sounded romantic, she liked the way he had taken her hand too, so she just grinned and nodded – they were going anyway, they might as well have fun.

The Monday before the trip there were ten staff off sick, then eleven the next day, so Alton Towers was cancelled. Worse still Alton Towers had never been re-arranged, despite many vague and open promises from staff to 'look into that one' or 'get something going there' the actual trip had never happened. They never knew whether they would be allowed on the rides or not.

When Tracy's Mum had said 'Alton Towers' about Tracy and George living together, it meant 'yeh, right!' or 'don't get your hopes up'. This infuriated Tracy, and she wished she knew more about what was involved so that she could show her Mum that this time she was wrong, this time she would get onto a roller coaster, this time the dream was going to be real.

Tracy phoned Tim again and arranged to go and see him on her own. George seemed to be busy doing other things at the moment, which was fine with Tracy for this visit. If George was not there then Tim could explain things faster, and write some of the details down for her so she could look through them by herself later.

She sat down on the same sofa.

"So, hey, Tracy. How's it going?"

"It's not."

Tim pursed his lips and nodded, "OK, yeh, I think I know what you mean there, but maybe you don't know enough about what is happening, huh, you know, the bits you're not noticing? How was it meeting George's Mum, for example?"

"I was really, really good. I think she hates me, but, after listening to Nicola I don't care any more."

"Well, there, that's brilliant. Can I ask you what you mean, you were really, really good?"

"I didn't get, well, sometimes see, Tim, I speak out, specially if I'm angry, and sometimes it makes things worse. Sometimes I hear my voice and what comes out isn't what I meant. I hurt people sometimes. I worked really hard and I didn't do that with George's Mum. Least ways not that visit."

"OK, I get what you're meaning there. Sometimes, though, I don't think it's a bad thing, it's something I admire about you actually, that you will speak out like that. I do think you were right to try not to that time with Mrs Sarandon, so, well done!"

Tracy liked Tim more now, although his enthusiasm for everything sometimes wound her up. She had started to relax about how much she could say to him.

"So, you're going round to George's house now I understand? That's something new I guess?"

"Yes, yes I guess it is. But it's not enough."

"No. I know. Listen Tracy, I need to ask you, with the way it's going at the moment with Mrs Sarandon, if a house comes up quite soon, would you be prepared to move on your own? Or would you even be willing to share a house with someone else, if things don't work out with George moving in?"

Tracy was speechless. She sat back into the sofa with a heavy sigh. She wished Tim had not said that. She tried to think about what this would mean, and how she would feel living on her own, or, worse still, with someone else. Then she thought about how George would feel if she lived with someone else, and shook her head. She could not do that to him, she knew it would break his heart. He would not go out with her if she moved in with someone else, she could see why too, she would feel the same if George moved in with anyone else.

"No, no way. Maybe if I moved by myself George could always come later, there would be room for him, but not with anyone else, no, never."

"OK Tracy, that's fine. The thing is though, you could not move into a two-bedroom house on your own. If we look for a house for you to move into on your own, we could only get a one-bedroom place. It might be quicker, but there wouldn't be room for George. If you want to live with George you'll have to wait for a two-bedroom house, for the two of you."

Tracy did not know what she could say, she felt herself flush deeply and hung her head to try and hide it. She had assumed that Tim had realised their intentions, she had assumed that because he had smiled at them holding hands he knew what they were wanting. Now she realised that she was going to have to explain it to him, and she did not think she could. It was all too embarrassing, and the illusion that Tim was all right and on their side was shattered. He might be shocked or angry, might turn into someone who told them they could not do this. Tracy wanted to cry. All of a sudden a wave of such sadness and disappointment, combined with embarrassment and an unwillingness to try and explain everything swept over her and she knew she had to get out or she really would start crying. She got up and with her head down and eyes looking straight at the floor, she said goodbye.

"Don't go! I know I said something wrong then, but please, don't just go, stay and help me understand, what is it? Please, Tracy!" Tim's voice grew fainter as she ran down the stairs.

Tracy was so annoyed with Tim for still not knowing what they wanted and annoyed with herself because she had assumed that he did, she had nearly said something to him. She knew she would have to be more careful about assuming people were going to be all right about her relationship with George.

While she was sitting on the bus Tracy realised she was assuming that George knew what living together would mean, and a moment of horror struck her as she realised George may also be assuming they would have a bedroom each. She needed to see him, to talk to him about her dream of them having a really big bed like her Mum's in one room, both of them sleeping together. She should have said something to George before, did he already know? What would he think of her if he did not?

Tim was annoyed with himself. He had said something or done something. Perhaps he should not have asked her about moving out by herself? But it had seemed like a good thing to ask, as she seemed to be such a strong, independent person. Tim wondered if he would have asked George the same question. He realised he ought to but probably would not have done.

*   *   *

George was ready, he was nervous, and he was trying to work out how to get Tracy to go for a walk in the park. They had both said to each other that they wanted to talk, and George had managed to persuade her to come into town on the bus with him. He had the most beautiful ring. He really did have no money now as it had cost everything he had, but it was the best ring in the shop, and he had it.

George had crept into Mum and Dad's room when they were out one evening and taken the tie that he had worn before. It was a special tie because it had a knot in it already and he just had to pull the clip over the top of his shirt. George liked this, and thought of it as his own tie really, Dad never seemed to wear it, and had said it was a 'special' one. George was used to the special things being for him. He was wearing it now, and seeing him in the suit and tie had made Tracy giggle a bit. Not in a bad way, she was not laughing at him, she was giggling in a good way, and he knew she really liked him in his suit and tie.

He had found a bench in the park when he had come on his own and bought the ring. It was underneath a tree, which had flowers on it at the moment. George thought it was a really magical place because although it was still really cold and the tree had no leaves on it, it was somehow covered in large white flowers which smelled strong and dropped petals on the bench. It made George smile to see the tree making flowers, as though it was doing it just for the two of them. He had known as soon as he saw it that this was the right place.

He had spent some time looking round and checking that he knew where it was and how to find it again. The bench had a wall behind it and a large bush on the other side of the path opposite, which meant not many people could see anyone sitting right in the middle. George liked this about it too as he did not want lots of people to see them so it really was the perfect place.

George insisted on them going for a walk in the park, and as they walked around to it, he asked her to sit down on his chosen bench. Then he stood in front of her and, shaking visibly, he took one of her hands in his own and knelt down on one knee.

It was not until this moment that Tracy had a clue what was going on, and she could not believe it. She looked at the picture he was creating around her . . . the bench, the tree, the suit, George kneeling down, and as she watched he took a small box from his pocket and opened it so she could see inside . . . a ring. It was true! This man, her man, the man she loved and who loved her, was going to ask her . . .

"Tracy, you know, will you marry me?"

He was smiling and the nerves made his smile crooked, the box with the ring was shaking in his hands. George adjusted his weight so he could hold the box in both hands. As he did so she took his hands and the box in her own and smiled at him.

"Yes, George, yes, I'll marry you. Oh my God, George! Do you mean it . . . Really?"

They hugged, and a sound exploded from George's chest which was part shout, part sob. He almost dropped the ring as his arms reached to hold her. She held him up and pulled him to sit on the bench next to him. Their heads touched as they both bent together over the small black velvet box. George took the ring and placed it on her finger. She had to correct him and get him to put it on the correct finger, and it fitted really well. All she could do was carry on whispering,

"Oh-my-God-do-you-mean-it-George? I mean really? You mean it? Oh my God."

He had no more room for words; George was full, so full of the best feeling in the world. He had done it, the right ring on the right bench with Tracy, the right woman, and he had done it.

Buying the ring had been easier than he had thought it would be in the end. He had got all his money together, and stood by himself at the bus stop. His Mum thought he was out with Tracy, and Tracy thought he was out with Susan. The bus trip had been fine, he knew it really well and there were other people getting off at the stop he wanted. It was not a big town centre, just a shopping precinct, cinema, a couple of cafés and the park.

There was a jewellers on Dunbas Street, round the corner from the high street. He went in and a tall woman with lots of make up came straight over to him.

"Hello there, what can we do for you?" Her voice was high and George was not sure who she meant by 'we', but he breathed deeply and looked her straight in the eye.

"I want to buy a ring, you know, for my girlfriend."

"Oh, my word." She giggled and looked round, "OK, well, yes . . . erm . . . how much money were you thinking of spending on this ring?"

"This is what I have." He held out both hands with all his coins in.

"Oh, OK, well come over here to the counter, dear, and we'll count that then shall we?"

He tipped all the money out onto the counter and she had leaned over it, counting and sorting it into piles as she went. Her voice was lower and quieter doing this, and George moved closer to watch. She was wearing strong perfume which he thought was a lovely smell, but it seemed to fill the whole room. He thought it was too strong for such a small space and did not want to get too close to her.

He could not remember how much she said he had in the end, but she got out a key and unlocked the counter in front of her.

"Right well, let's see, that means you can afford any of these on trays A through to D."

Her voice was high and loud again. She picked up two small trays full of rings and put them out on the counter in front of him.

"Which one takes your fancy out of these then?"

They looked amazing, all lined up together, George found it difficult to see each one rather than just the tray full. She bent down again and lifted out two more trays, as she stood up and placed them next to the others he saw it. It was beautiful, not so glittery as some of them, with very small stones set into the ring, not held up in a cage like the others.

"Now of course these aren't real gold, or real diamonds for that matter, but I think that for under fifty pounds these are some of the best you'll find. That one?"

George had stepped forward and was trying to pick up the ring he wanted.

"Really? Well, it's an unusual one certainly. Let me see if I can get that out for you so you can see it properly."

"It's that one, I know it. Is it OK? The money, it's enough?"

"Oh, yes, no problem there . . . " She pulled the ring out of the tray and handed it to George, " . . . y ou'll have a little change to take home as well."

"I want it. Can it be, you know, in a little box? Does it cost more?"

"No, no that's fine, I'll get a box and we can wrap it for you as well if you like?"

George thought for a moment.

"You mean in paper like a present?"

"Yes, wrapping paper of your choice, we have a small selection."

"No, I want it to be, you know, so I can open it," he mimed opening the box in front of her, "and she can see it like that."

"OK, so, just straight like that then? OK, shall I just take it out of here?" She pointed to the neat piles of his money. George simply nodded and she took what she needed. There was not much left, but there was enough for the bus. This was a relief, he had not thought to make sure he had his bus fare.

On the journey home George had grinned all the way, and held onto the small black box in his pocket all the way. It really had been that easy, and he had phoned Tracy as soon as he got in.

George realised now that until he asked her he had not thought that Tracy might have said no. In the small silence as she had breathed in to answer him, as he had adjusted his weight, he had felt himself suspended, floating and falling in a dream land, waiting for the sound that would make the world breathe again. And she had said it, she had said yes.

Tracy was crying and as he looked at her, eyes bright, red nosed and leaning towards him, holding her hand so she could see the ring, he knew that this was the greatest moment of his life. He alone had made this happen, it was better than fighting giants, better than rescuing her from a cave, this was real, and he was really going to marry Tracy!

*   *   *

Just as she had started to feel as though she might want to play something else on the computer, something had happened in the game Susan had never seen before. This new creature, this winged lion whatever it was, was not mentioned anywhere in all the information that came with the game, nor was it mentioned at all on the Internet site. She had even tried looking on the *Nephillim Caves* discussion forum. Some players had discovered that shooting at the feet wiped out the giants, but none of them mentioned anything about dreaming that angels had told them to. Susan had not mentioned it either, so she had no idea if anyone else had shared the dream. It was all too weird for it to be just her and George, but it was all too weird to talk about.

No one in any of the chat channels had made any mention of red, flying, sabre-toothed lions, which could be healed with purple gemstones. She had really hoped for some hints and tips about that, or at least some others who were asking about it. She had not expected there to be no mention at all.

Come to think of it, Susan realised looking back at the computer screen, where a live chat was slowly scrolling upwards as people spoke, no one mentioned the purple jewels either, and she wondered if any of them had found them. It seemed unlikely that she should have done something so obvious before anyone else, but she thought it would be easier to ask about that than about the lion itself.

She sat back in front of the computer and tapped in the instructions for joining the chat channel again. This one was called 'The Nephillim Cave', and the chat was just about this one game.

[Connected] Suzy_Saran has entered chat, welcome back!
[Suzy_Saran] Hey, you guys found the purple stones in the fifth cavern amongst the food? Don't eat the giant's food eh? Vomit City

or what!

[Dangerboy] No kidin suzy, tried that ages ago :¬{}~~~ Barf City

[phyrphox] Hey Suzy, no, not got that far yet, what are they used for . . . not the kind of game for jewels is it??

[Suzy_Saran]I know. Not sure what they're for yet, but you pick up everything eh? Yah Never Know!

[Dangerboy] can't think they're any use. Typical girl collecting jewels, eh.

[lotysox]oh naff off, not so dangerous boy. Pathetic dig at the girls, wnaker. Take no notice suzy, he's jealous, none of us are at the 5th cavern yet . . . congrats & ta for tip . . . will look for jewels when I get there.

[phyrphox]/me doesn't understand . . . did I miss, what 5th cavern

[Dangerboy] dangerboy twats loty . . . learn to type before giving out WANKER

[phyrphox] calm down boys godsakes, whatsup? Just 'cos suzy's good . . . what's 5th cavern suzy?

[lotysox]yup, all the time, brings more relief than naffy caves

[Suzy_Saran]info-over guys, who needs to? Phyrphox - 5th cavern I came to giants nest has purple jewels and food to pick up. Don't eat food,:¬{}~~ but any clue on jewels use?

[phyrphox] not got to any caverns, maybe took different turns, just caves and giants and got to a waterfall yesterday . . . went back, now ammo high from foot-shooting.

[Dangerboy] waterfall? . . . there's no waterfall, i've been right through these caves, i should know. Jewels prob worthless.

[Suzy_Saran] ok outahere, Dangerboy is too big for this room, bye. [end] . . .

Susan hated some of the guys who hung around in the chat rooms. She had been in one with Dangerboy before, and he had been just as arrogant then. It felt good to know something he did not. It was obvious none of them had any idea about the red lion. It was interesting what phyrphox had said about a waterfall, Susan wondered what she would have done. She had never turned round and gone back throughout the game. Nor had she tried any of the other cave entrances that were not going in the one direction she had been heading in. It surprised her that phyrphox could have not come to any other caverns at all when she had found five. They must have all gone different ways.

What she was unsure about was what she was supposed to do with the lion. Having been unable to kill it, and having now healed it by accident, it did not leave Oemor alone. Also there had been no more giants since then. She had got the gun, knife and c-cylinder back off the ground.

. . . and come to think of it, she realised that was another strange thing, Susan had not known Oemor had a knife there at all, it had felt as though he had done that all by himself. He had responded really well earlier to shooting the giants' feet once she had written in the journal about her dream. Susan wanted them to have a two-way dialogue . . . but how? She had tried to get the the *Nephillim Caves* master com she had wanted, but since That Damn Meal, what else could she do?

Of course! She could hear him when he shouted out her name every time he had died. Except one time, after That Damn Meal, she had been angry and played the same scene over and over to vent her anger. He had died over and over. She remembered now, in the end, he had cried out the word 'No'. Perhaps he could learn to control his voice more? Learn to talk?

Susan jumped slightly at the thought. Was that possible? There was only one way to find out. She logged out of the chat channel and logged off the Internet connection. When she started up *Nephillim Caves* she did not go into the game, instead she went straight into her gaming journal. If she could communicate with Oemor at all, it would have to be through this.

"1st March. How are you feeling today Susan?"
She clicked on 'End Questions' and chose the 'Journal entry' option instead.

. . . "Oemor, I have heard you calling out my name, it is very loud! I'm assuming it is you, but I can hear you really clearly. One time I heard you shouting out 'no!' and I worried about what was happening. Since then I have heard nothing. I know you are still

coming to save me, but I wonder how you are and what is happening, I think every day about how you must be thinking and what you are feeling. I'm sure that if you spoke out loud I would be able to hear every word, I hear everything else that happens, the calling of the Nephillim, the shrieking noise they make when you kill them. At least, I imagine that is what the terrible noise is. I picture you with your gun . . . I can hear the gun loudly, Oemor . . . killing everything that stands in your way. I would love it if you would speak to me, my love, and tell me all your thoughts, every day, I want to know how you are." . . .

She clicked on 'save and exit'.

This was the first time she had written in the journal as though she really was the gaming character he was coming to rescue. It was a short entry for her, but she could not think of anything else to say. It did not seem to fit to tell him about school today, which was boring anyway. She had not thought very much before about any connection between Oemor and what she put in the journal. If he somehow really knew what she wrote, she thought he must be so bored. It was filled with all her stupid ideas about school and Mr Sullivan and how much she hated Mum and how George was getting on.

Susan lay on her bed and wondered about the character, how the programming might work. Did he think? Or have processes which resulted in thought? What would he think about? Did Oemor know the fairy-tale story? If he thought at all she realised he probably must at least know that. Which would mean he thought her Mum was dead. What must he think of her now then, if she had told him all about her? Susan just had to be able to communicate with him properly and find out how much he knew . . . what exactly did 'sentient program' mean? Did he know he was just a game? Did he know she was really out here and not chained up in there? She got up and started the game straight away, wondering if it had worked and whether there was a way she could write in the journal while playing the game.

Oemor was still in the cavern with the lion, which had been following him round as he picked up various odd-looking things, ate some food and rested. He had wanted to offer it food, but had been unable to. It did not seem to be worth the effort to fight against his own body just to be nice to this thing. The lion made him uneasy and he was unsure what to do with it. He was aware that he knew a bit more about Susan, and was astonished to realise that she had been able to hear him! He had called out her name, that was true, and he had fought to say something else when he had died another time. It had certainly never occurred to him that she could hear him, and everything else . . . his gun firing and everything. He felt close to her now, really connected, and happy, yes he felt happy, that she knew for certain he was coming to get her. He tried to speak, but nothing happened. He tried again, really hard, he tried to do it as he had done when he died, shouting out loud in a moment of panic. He pushed at the inside of his throat with his mind and threw his head back.

All that happened was he breathed out noisily.

It was frustrating but he was not sure what else he could do, and he so wanted to speak to Susan, he was determined he would speak to her or die trying. As he thought this, he realised, just before he died was the only time he had ever spoken.

He tried again, and suddenly he could not move, at all; arms, legs, head, nothing, he was completely frozen. This had happened to him once or twice before and it scared him more than any giant. He could not breathe. He knew he had just taken a breath to try speaking, so he pushed with all his might against his chest to push it out. As he stayed there unable to move Oemor found that he could bring more of himself into the effort of speech as he did not have to put any effort into standing up or holding the gun. He pushed himself fully up through his throat, feeling exactly now as he did whenever he died, that final cry wrenching the life out of him. He was using the fear he felt from being unable to move to push breath with a new sense of panic.

He heard a frustratingly low moan.

Considering the effort he was putting in to squeeze his entire being out towards his mouth, rendered immobile and uncaring of anything else, driven by fear and determination, the noise that came from him sounded pathetic. There was no way she could hear that.

He had to really concentrate and make this thing work. Frozen in time and space he pushed again with all his might, knowing that by rights he should be falling over and dropping everything, he pushed everything he had into making a sound, a bigger sound, a better sound.

All he heard was a wheezing breath of her name, "Suuuuuuuuuuuuuuuueeeeeeeeeeeeeeee"

He had done it. He was exhausted.

Susan was stunned. She had put the game on pause to see if she could start the gaming journal and write to Oemor while she was playing, and he had moaned once and had then almost said her name out loud. While the game was paused! She realised it must pause his body but not his mind. This was amazing. She had paused the game to suggest that he sit down and try to do it by relaxing and letting the sound out gently, he had clearly been trying to scream. Screaming was the only speech he knew so it made sense it would be what he would try. But now the game was paused and he was clearly still trying, and succeeding, to actually say something, to say her name of his own accord, not as part of the scripted program.

Now Susan did not know what to do. Should she carry on and try writing and see if he responded, leave him to carry on, or take him off pause? She decided to leave him and see if she could get in to the gaming journal. It did not occur to Susan to wonder what 'Pause' might be like for a computer program that was learning to think for itself and remaining conscious the whole time. Had she thought about it she may have done something else. As it was she left Oemor standing, frozen, unable to move for ten minutes while she found out how to start up, write in, save and exit her gaming journal. As it turned out, the noise he made when she took him off pause and finally released him taught her more about his experience than she could ever have gained from sitting and thinking about it.

Oemor had been terrified. He had started to believe he would be trapped in the living hell of immobility for the rest of his life. His only hope seemed to be that Susan might hear him if he made a noise.

He had been exhausted by calling her name, and it had seemed so quiet he was sure she could not have heard him at all. He remained stuck for such a long time he had managed to recover from his effort and had tried again. He was in the middle of pushing his entire life's energy through himself and out of his mouth when Susan pressed the 'Pause' button a second time and released him into movement.

What he heard was a piercing shriek of pain, eerily similar to the cry of the Nephillim as they died, and the word that was flung from his mouth was the only one that made any sense to him,

"HEEEEEEEEEEEELLLLLLLLLLLPPPPPPPPPPPPPPPPP!!!!!!!!!!"

He gasped for breath and fell to the floor, realising that he could move now, or at least he could have if the cry had not taken all his strength and power from him.

Oemor lay exhausted on the rocky ground and realised that he somehow knew that Susan had heard him trying to speak, just now, just before he had been frozen. If she had by some miracle heard the breath he had so unsuccessfully pushed from his body, she must have heard his cry for help ringing soundly in her ears! This was strange, she seemed to think he needed to relax and let the noise come in a different way to shouting it.

Whenever Oemor had fallen down the shaft and been back at the beginning, it had felt as though he had learned to walk, almost as though he did not know how to. He had felt his own body try and sit himself up time and time again, felt himself slow right down, felt his movements analysed and responded to. He had been unable to control the experience, but he had certainly felt it. This meant that Oemor knew how to learn something new. He knew how to slow down and pay attention to every stage, how each small movement was either right or wrong, and how to learn to only do the things that helped. He had sat up, he had walked, in the end he had felt himself sitting up and walking quite well.

Oemor had also learned how to gain control of his own body from that experience, he had learned to pull himself through what his body was doing, learned to stretch himself outside of the control on his hands and legs to get what he wanted. Oemor sat up now, with a smooth ease and leant his back against the rock face. He breathed in and started to find out how to learn to speak, in the same way that he had found out how to learn, slowly and precisely. He relaxed as Susan suggested, and tried to gently allow a noise to come out of his mouth. He wanted Susan to know he was all right, he knew she had heard him shout for help and now did not know what was happening. This was his driving force, which kept him going, over and over with a self-imposed calm he did not feel, so he could say out loud that he was all right really.

All the time the horned lion was hovering next to him, watching and clearly waiting. It made no reaction to the strange noises he started to make, its wings flapped monotonously keeping the huge feet a metre off the ground, its tail, now completely healed, lashed gently from side to side behind it. The lion gazed down at Oemor and waited, silently, for the action to begin again.

Chapter 9

Tracy realised that being engaged to George might just be the way that Tim could understand why she had been so annoyed with him without her having to explain it to him. Surely, if they were to get married, then he was bound to work out that they just wanted one bedroom.

Following the giddy excitement in the park after George had proposed, they had gone for hot chocolate in the café nearby. They started to calm down and talked about who to tell, how to tell them and tried guessing their reactions.

George had changed over the last two months, he seemed stronger and clearer about what he wanted and how to get it. She thought he was standing taller, looking people in the eye more, and definitely talking more. Tracy loved him all the more with this new-found confidence. The George she had known last year would never have managed to take her to the park in his suit and propose. She had no idea where the ring had come from, or how he had got it, but it had become clear to her as they talked that George had managed all of this without anyone knowing. Even his sister, Susan, who she thought he told everything to, had not known.

Tracy had wanted to ask him how he got the ring but it seemed rude to question the gift in any way. Instead she asked another question on her mind,

"So, George, what's going on with you? You seem different, more . . . well, more. You're bigger than you were, stronger.

George flushed and looked proud, which Tracy liked even more. It was a look she had rarely seen on his face, and had never seen outside the kitchen.

He told her a story about a King and his daughter, how she had been taken by her evil brother and trapped in some caves, and how her lover was fighting giants to come and save her.

"That doesn't make any sense, I mean, it's a story an'all, but I asked why you're bigger now."

"Yeh, I know, you know? But, I have to tell you what I did, which was wrong. It's Sue's computer game, it's the story. But then when you play it, Tracy . . . you should feel it, it's amazing you know? You can feel your heart beating fast, and it makes you sweat and breathe heavy. It's exciting, and the giants are really huge and frightening, you just have to shoot and shoot till they go. You have to learn to run fast and shoot a gun, and I feel, you know, more than I feel."

Tracy had never been interested in computers for anything but typing. She loved to see her own words looking neat and printed out. Apart from that Tracy always thought of computer games as something just for boys. If Susan had one though, they must be for girls as well. She had seen the computer games George played at College and had felt annoyed that he was doing such childish things, it was not like him, she had never understood why he went to the class. Now she saw him and heard him talking about this computer it started to make sense why he wanted to learn about them.

"So, could I? Could I have a go?"

"Sue said she'd kill me if I went near it again. I wasn't supposed to, you know? It was a bad thing for me to go into her room and play with it. I'll never be allowed, you know? Not now."

"Well, what about at College? You go on computers there."

"No, Tracy, this is nothing like the College ones, nothing at all. It's just not the same."

"Oh. That's a shame. Really."

They sat in silence for a while, and the conversation moved back to the list of people they wanted to tell about their engagement.

"Tim. We should tell Tim, for the house and stuff. And 'cos I think he likes us."

"Yeh, I know," George was grinning again, "We're not seeing him though for . . . I don't know when. Maybe we could, you know, ring?"

"Oh yeh, let's do it now, there's a phone here. Have you got any change, money like coins left?"

They both felt unsure about telling their parents, both knowing that there would be a lot of shouting and anger. They decided it would be better not to tell anyone until they had seen Tim. He might be able to help them tell the people who were important.

Tracy talked a bit about her Mum, but was careful not mention her father. Marriage or no marriage, she was not ready for George to know about him yet. If she did leave home and move in with George, it would take her Dad a while to realise, he came round so rarely these days. She knew her Dad had a new girlfriend, Tracy hoped he would have another child with her, a child that was not disabled, that would take him safely out of her life without George ever knowing him. She knew he would hit George really hard if he ever did meet him.

As George had never even met her Mum, they decided he would visit a few days after Tracy had told her. They figured this would give her Mum some time to get used to the idea so she would at least be polite to him.

George's family was a different matter altogether. They knew Susan would be all right, George seemed to think it had been her idea in the first place, but they did not know about his Mum. Tim had visited and met her now. George did not know what had been said, she had not talked to him about it at all.

Tim was the only person who seemed to take their relationship seriously in any way. They had finished their hot chocolates and held hands at the bus stop, each grinning into space, feeling a new thrill of excitement and fear at returning to their homes as engaged people.

*   *   *

There was a slight pause. So slight that Tracy and George did not notice it, but Tim did.

"Well, congratulations you two! Wow, this is amazing."

He shook George vigorously by the hand and leaned over to peck Tracy on the cheek.

"Yes, wow, well, come in, come in. Sit yourselves down, yes, gosh, you won't be so shy about holding hands any more eh? So, have you plans for the big day? Do you know when it's going to be? Can I get you a drink? Nothing stronger than tea here I'm afraid, but still, can I get you something? "

He was rambling, filling the room with noise so they could not hear the still silence that surrounded them. He concentrated hard on trying to do everything exactly as he would if it had been anyone else. It felt like a performance, a travesty, almost as though he was acting out a part in a play and was suddenly unsure of his lines. Why? Tim could not think why was it so different for these two? Why should he react so differently to an engagement? Was he really that prejudiced still?

Looking at their glowing faces he could see how important this was to both of them, and he also knew it could help them with getting a house together if they were married.

It was not until after they had left and he had a chance to think about it properly that he finally realised what it was he had said to upset Tracy on her last visit. Tim had clumsily assumed that two people would want a two-bedroom house. He tutted to himself and shook his head, typical social worker, he thought, just count the numbers and ignore the people.

For now he was not sure how Mrs Sarandon would react to the news of their marriage, she was so clear that she had a special son who needed to be looked after. He had had a reasonably successful visit with her a couple of weeks earlier, and was due to visit again with Mrs Barnaby next week. Mrs Sarandon had been clear that she had to look after George for the rest of her life and had remained unmoved by any of his arguments about adulthood and independence and moving on. The only glimmer of hope had been when she had mentioned watching George cook a meal recently; she had not realised George could cook like that. He had tried to press this point to emphasise George's abilities.

"Don't be ridiculous," she'd said, "Roasting a chicken does not mean someone like my George can just up and move away from home, away from his family."

Tim found that this was always the hardest and the most crucial stage with these conversations, when he tried to explain that no one lived without the support that they needed. George would still have the care he needed to live safely and healthily; it just would not all come from his mother all the time.

Tim knew that he had done his best, and he knew that it had not been enough. He also knew that it rarely was the first time, or the second, or even the third. He would like to be able to speak some words of magic which would inspire parents to suddenly see the world from a new point of view, but he knew it did not happen that way. He also knew that it was more down to George and what he said to his Mum than anything Tim could ever do. Thinking it through he knew that getting engaged to Tracy would move things along, he just did not know in what direction. As they spoke Tim saw that they had a new determination, in both of them, but particularly in George. Whether this was because they were getting to know him or because George was in fact changing he did not know.

They had been excited and wanted to talk some more about getting a house together, this time with a much more practical view, discussing which area of the town they would prefer, what type of place they would be looking for. Tim realised that this clear vision they had would be what they would need to keep going through the long, drawn-out process ahead of them. The more they talked in real terms about it actually happening the less likely they were to give up and retreat into a state of despair.

The couple had surprisingly similar ideas about what their house would be like inside. From their joyful discussions, Tim assumed they had not talked about these things before. George was clear and specific about everything to do with the kitchen, what type of oven, where it would be in relation to the cupboards and work surfaces, and that the sink would be under a window so he could look out while washing up. Tracy was clear and specific about everything to do with the bedroom and bathroom, where the bed would be placed, how big the wardrobe should be, and what colour she wanted in the bathroom. Even down to where the taps should be placed, George and Tracy shared their daydreams and ideas about what their shared house would look like in more detail than Tim had heard before. This was more attention to detail than Tim had paid to any house he had moved into.

They seemed happy and relaxed talking with him in this way. He felt pleased that they were trusting him, and they were calm and comfortable when he finally interrupted their reverie.

"So, what do your parents make of all this?"

"They don't know anything," said Tracy.

"No, we wanted to tell you, for you to be, you know, the first to know."

Tim was surprised and flattered.

"So . . . " George looked down, "How do I tell her, my Mum, that I want to marry Tracy, without her shouting, like she does?"

"George," Tracy took his hand as she spoke, "We have to tell her that we're going to get married, not just that you want to. I mean, I want to as well, and we will."

They blushed and smiled shyly to each other, then both looked at Tim for the answer.

"Gee, guys, I mean, really, George, mate, to be honest, I don't know that she won't shout, I mean, she probably will. The question for you is how much is that going to matter to you. What I mean is, you could try and make sure she doesn't get upset, that would be best probably," Tim stood up and paced to the window and back, his head down, deep in thought as he spoke, "But, to be honest, I don't really know how. I mean, really, she's gonna shout. Part of me thinks you might as well just tell her anyway."

George looked at him, that straight gaze which Tim found unnerving. Neither of them spoke.

"I don't know." He carried on, "I guess my only real feeling is that whatever you say you should do it together. But then, Tracy, if your Mum hasn't met George yet that would be a bit of a shock for her . . . to meet him as your fiancée for the first time. But then, I guess, that it's true though isn't it? Unless you're going to meet her and not tell her, but then if she found out you got engaged later, then she would know you had lied to her. I don't know, Tracy, maybe you should tell her on your own first?

But your family, George, if you want my advice, for what it's worth, I think Tracy should go with you so you don't have to tell them on your own. I guess it won't be too bad, I mean, they already know you're moving in together . . . you never know, she might be pleased you're making an honest woman of her!"

Tim was not convinced they would understand the joke, but as they both blushed and giggled he guessed they must have done.

"OK," said George, "Thanks, Tim. Maybe we will, you know? Tracy can come with me." He grinned and squeezed her hand before turning back to Tim,

"You've met her now, my Mum, you know, you came to see her

when I wasn't there, and she talked to you. She's meeting Nicola's Mum is that right?"

"Yes, yes that's right, George, Mrs Barnaby is going to come with me next week. She sometimes visits parents to talk to them about what it was like for her when Nicola moved out." Tim looked at his watch and then spread his arms wide as he came back over to them.

"OK, right, well you two, that's it I'm afraid. I have to get on now, I'm meeting someone else. So, let me know how you get on OK? And we'll be in touch. Talk to your parents, let them know they can ring me if they want to, and I'll see you next week after that second visit with your Mum, George, OK? All right then, and congratulations once again, well done! I'm very happy for both of you. Tell me about your plans for the wedding next time, OK?"

George and Tracy left, grinning and holding hands. As they walked out and heard Tim's last words they caught each other's eye . . . the wedding? They had not talked about a wedding at all. They had talked a lot about being engaged, and a bit about being married, which was all about the house and living together. Neither of them had thought much about an actual wedding.

"Wow, Tracy, we need to talk about that a lot! What are you doing?"

"I have to go home now, but I'll see you tomorrow at the centre, we're going to College OK?"

"OK," George said, "I want to tell Susan when I see her, I didn't see her yesterday at all, but I don't want to see her and not tell her. I'll tell her not to tell Mum. I can ask her to come in and sit with us when you come and we tell Mum, OK?"

"Yes . . . I want to meet this sister of yours, I've heard a lot about her."

"OK, you will. I love you, Tracy, I'll see you tomorrow."

They kissed outside Tim's offices and then headed off in different directions. George could walk to his house from there, and Tracy had a bus to catch.

Chapter 10

Oemor had lost all concept of time. He had no idea how long he had been in the caves, or how long it was since he had started to learn to talk. He knew that Susan had a different idea of time passing to him, she talked about days passing that he had no memory of.

Susan's references to the days getting longer and spring approaching, when only four days ago she had complained about the ice and snow indicated time must be different for her. This meant that either Susan was thinking about an imaginary life locked away in some cavern quite close to here, or that something strange was happening to him and the way time worked. Either way, he was not sure anymore, he just kept on going, to rescue her.

Oemor wandered the caves unhindered save for the lion which silently followed him everywhere. The lion often flew towards cave entrances which were in a different direction to the way he was headed. It always went to the right of where he wanted to go. Always, so far, Oemor had continued in the same direction he had always headed in and the lion had followed after him.

These last few hours felt as though he had been going around in circles. The repetitive nature of the caves and rock surface meant it all looked very similar, but this cave he had just stepped into looked exactly the same as one he had already been in. He could tell because he had just glanced round to see the lion suspended in the air in front of another entrance where the caves forked into two. It was the same scene he had glanced round at the last time the caves had forked, which was, by any measurement, hours ago. The outline of the rock face, the position of the lion . . . it really was *exactly* the same.

Oemor stopped. He must have been going round in circles, which must mean he should go down the other tunnel to stop, otherwise he would be stuck here forever. As he walked back towards the lion it fluttered its wings unusually, and set off down the tunnel in front of him for the first time. It was almost as though the lion had clear ideas about which way he should be heading, and had been trying to let Oemor know for some time.

The lion travelled swiftly through the air barely moving his wings at all and Oemor had to jog to keep up. The tunnel took a sharp turn to the left and was slopping downwards slightly, which meant jogging to keep up was easier. As they went the lion flew past an area of rock face, which was shimmering, and Oemor wanted to stop. He was all right for ammo, but low on food and first aid, so he wanted to stop to see what was in there. The lion swept past the rock face and onwards, Oemor slowed to a halt to shove his fist quickly in. He was lucky, it was food for himself. He turned and ran to catch up with the lion, and finally realised that his only way to get it to slow down was to say something, so he tried,

"Wait."

He ran and turning the next corner he realised the lion had stopped and waited for him. At least, he thought it had been for him. When he caught up though he came to another fork in the tunnels, where the lion had turned towards him and was waiting for him. From one of the tunnels, the one on the right . . . the one the lion was floating in front of, there was a curious noise. It was not a noise that Oemor knew very well, it had a faint, old familiarity to it which he could not place. It was not a noise he had heard in the caves before. It was a constant hissing noise, sometimes higher, sometimes lower in tone, almost a rumbling sound. As he turned to the tunnel entrance where the noise was coming from, the lion also turned and headed straight down it, and Oemor followed. He was unclear about the lion and not sure why he had shouted for it to wait for him. He had not had a companion on his journey so far, but the lion was different and very strange. It had a presence and having hung around behind him this far it seemed as clear as anything could be that it wanted him to follow it in this direction.

As they carried on down the tunnel it was obvious they were getting closer to whatever it was that made the noise . . . it was getting much louder and Oemor also started to feel something he had not felt for a very long time indeed – he felt the air moving around him. He could hear it in his ears and had to hold the gun still consciously to stop it being blown slightly in his loose hold. This was odd, but gave Oemor a strange combination of hope and dread. A breeze could only mean an exit of some sort. That would mean he had been led out of the caves, which was a relief, but also led away from Susan. He would never leave the caves without her. If it was a way out, he would remember where it was, then go back for Susan. Then they could leave straight away, as soon as they were together.

The lion was out of sight, it had gone round another bend. Oemor jogged to catch up. As he rounded the sharp bend he almost collided with it, and nearly fell straight down the sheer drop that was in front of him. He reached out to gain his balance instinctively and actually grabbed the flesh of the lion. Surprisingly it did not move at all, and so he was able to regain his balance easily. He looked down at the fall in front of him, which was clearly the source of the noise and the movement in the air. It was not an opening to the outside at all, quite the opposite. This was a shaft going straight downwards, deep into the heart of the rock, and it had a flood of water pouring over it, stirring the air and sounding impenetrably loud all around him. It was both exhilarating and frightening. The water was falling at great speed, the drop was long and seemingly endless. There was clearly no other way to go, this was the only direction the tunnel went in – straight down or back the way he came. Back to going round in circles he thought.

No, there had been another way, a different tunnel before this one. As Oemor turned to go back and try the other way, the lion swept overhead, passed him and descended in front of him slowly so he could clearly see its paws with talons and fur visible before his eyes. It came down closer to him than it had been before, and spread its wings from one rock face to the other, completely blocking his way. He would have to push past the thing in order to leave the waterfall. He stopped in front of it, waited for a little while and then slowly turned and faced the water again. He made a movement as if to go back and then, as the lion rose to come in front of him, he dashed passed it, under the huge talons. He ran as fast as he could.

He had not been fast enough, his feet were not touching the ground at all, he was going through the physical motions of running but in fact he was floating in the air and going nowhere. He looked up and realised that the lion had caught his leather tunic in its talons and was, eagle-like, carrying him with great sweeping beats of its wings, back down the tunnel and right out over the waterfall. When he was above the centre of rushing, tumbling water, the lion let go.

Oemor was falling. He was falling very fast, and was battered and beaten by the water, which seemed to be falling faster than he was. Oemor had no idea what would happen, he did not know what to do in water.

Eventually Oemor was completely submerged. He was being pushed further down underwater by the weight of the waterfall landing on top of him. Oemor could feel pressure building up inside his chest, he did not know what to do, his heartbeat was dangerously fast, he was terrified and felt helpless, almost as though all he could do was just watch himself drown. His vision started to blur and everything around him went red, increasingly out of focus until he could see nothing, he had no oxygen in his body and, finally, he died.

*   *   *

Susan was walking home from school as usual, preferring to be by herself than standing up on the school bus. The walk was pleasant and it always gave her a chance to think about the game and what was happening. Today she was dwelling on school and, in particular, Mr Sullivan's class. He had jeans on for the first time today, brand new black ones, so they looked smart, but they were still jeans. Susan wondered if the teachers were really supposed to wear them when the students were not allowed to; she thought probably not. She grinned to herself that he had worn them anyway. He had a scruffy old jacket which he had taken off during the lesson, the early spring sun had been shining straight onto his desk, so he must have been pretty warm.

On the back row, where she was, it had been pretty chilly, it was too early in the year for the sun to get that far round the classroom. She liked the way he looked when he turned to write on the blackboard. With the sun at that angle his blue shirt had lit up from the inside and she could clearly see the outline of his shoulder and arm muscles. He was quite beautiful and she had enjoyed sitting at the back and looking at him. He seemed strong and his deep voice echoed around the room with a passion she did not hear from her other teachers.

Today he had been talking about the difference between a Jew and a Christian, and the two testaments in the Bible. They were supposed to be moving on to the New Testament after half-term. As she crossed the road and took the path down to the river, it occurred to her that Mr Sullivan might even be Jewish, not Christian. She stopped on the path, why had she never thought of that before? Did it really matter? She walked on. Not really, she thought, it was just amazing to realise she always assumed everyone would be Christians.

Her mind wandered back to the game, and how Oemor was getting on. He had done it, he had really learned to talk. It did not seem possible, but she had heard him ask the lion to wait for him.

Susan was not sure if it had been him at first, it was the first calm word she had heard him say. She had left him to it after he had sat down and started to really work at talking. All he was doing was just making a whole range of noises to himself and she had got bored. She had left the game running though, she thought if she turned it off he would never be able to get past where he was. After that night, it seemed to be all he tried to do. There were no giants to shoot, and just empty caves to walk around in. She had not paused the game since he had screamed out at her, so when she was not there she either left him sitting somewhere or turned it off properly. It was only a week later, and he had spoken clearly and calmly to the lion, like he had always been able to talk.

*   *   *

"You're what? You've done what? That's impossible, George, it's out of the question, no bloody way! Of course not."

She was towering over George and Tracy, who were huddled together on the sofa. Their faces were turned upwards, mouths slightly open. George's Mum was pointing down at them, her left hand clinging to her hip.

"I should bloody well think not! There's no way, absolutely no way at all. Is this some kind of joke? First you say you want to live together, then you say you're getting married!! George, what on earth has got into you these days? For Godsakes, you must be bloody joking. This is ridiculous and it's got to stop."

She kept on shouting because she knew if she calmed down she would cry. George took a breath as though he was going to try and say something.

" . . . Never you mind saying anything, I don't know how you've got the nerve."

Her finger moved to bear down on Tracy.

" . . . And as for you, what have you done to my son? You Hussy! I'm his mother! He lives here, this is his home, he cannot get married, Christ he can't even read, how the hell can he get married?"

Her face was close to Tracy's now and as she turned to her son she stood back up again and waved her hand at the ceiling.

"You can't even read, George! How are you going to sign your name? What will you live off? It's just ridiculous, this whole thing is some kind of fucking cruel joke."

She turned her face to the roof and drew breath.

"SUSAN! Susan! get down here right now."

"What, Mum, I'm busy." They could hear that Susan was running downstairs as she spoke.

"Did you know about this?"

"About what?

"Well if you came downstairs like I damn well told you to you'd bloody know wouldn't you. These two here, do you know what he's gone and done now? Do you know about this?"

The look she gave George told her Mum everything before Susan spoke.

"Oh. George . . . erm . . . yes, he told me last night, Mum. Hi. Are you Tracy?"

Susan stepped between her mother and Susan, and held her hand out. Her Mum stood open mouthed and stunned momentarily into silence at her daughter's calm politeness.

Susan and Tracy shook hands; Tracy did not manage to say

anything and Susan took a seat on the arm of the sofa next to George. She put her hand on his shoulder and when he looked up, she winked at him.

Her Mum saw the wink.

"I knew it, well if you knew about it, why the hell didn't you tell them how ridiculous it all is."

"Because I don't think it is ridiculous, Mum, I think George is really in love, he's twenty-nine years old and he wants to get married. Just 'cos they've got too many chromosomes between them doesn't mean none of that's true, it just makes it way more complicated for them. I didn't tell you because of what you just said – you'd try and stop them!"

"Complicated! *Complicated!!* You think that's all this is? . . . "

"Yeh, and I think you're making it way more *complicated* for them right now."

"I might have bloody known you'd take his side . . . any side as long as it was against me, right Susan?"

She tried to tower above Susan, pulling herself up to her full height, folding her arms tightly across her chest as she spoke and peered down her nose at her daughter.

"Oh for chrissakes, Mum, don't be so daft! It's George, and he's my older brother as well as your son. He doesn't need you using him to take sides."

Susan's voice was calming, and her Mum felt disconcerted, this had never happened to her. Her rights as George's mother were clear cut and fundamental. It made no sense that suddenly anyone, let alone her own family, were arguing against her.

"Look," Susan continued, "I know I fight with you, but really . . . this isn't about us, it's about George. Look at him, look what you're doing to him, Mum, you can't make him choose between his home and her. And anyway he's chosen her already."

"Can I go on your computer?"

George had been prepared for the shouting. He had known it would happen. Susan had warned him too, they both knew she was going to kick off. Somehow having Tracy sitting there made it all different. Usually he let the shouting wash over him, his mum always spoke too fast for him to follow. Sitting there on the sofa with Tracy right up close next to him, he heard every word, and tried to imagine what Tracy must think of it all. He had told Tracy that she would shout, and Tracy had still wanted to come and be with him. Now he felt ashamed and embarrassed.

George wanted to say something, he wanted his Mum to be quiet so he could say something, but there seemed to be no stopping her, and now Susan was here, they both just talked as though he and Tracy were not in the room. He glanced at Tracy to see what she thought. Tracy was watching his sister avidly, every word, every gesture, she did not give him or his Mum a second glance.

It took a short while for everyone to realise there was silence, and Tracy had asked a question.

"What? Erm . . . yeh, I guess so, later on," Susan paused, "It's a bit tricky at the moment, but . . . yeh, sure, why not. But Tracy, listen, do you know how you're going to get enough money for you and George to live together? I mean, I know Tim has said you can use housing benefit to pay rent, and there are housing associations who rent to people with learning disabilities like you, but then, will that pay for heating, lighting . . . " She started counting off on her fingers as she spoke, " . . . council tax, water rates, TV licence, food and everything else, I mean . . . how will the two of you actually live? If you can explain that, or if Tim can explain it to Mum, I think she might feel a bit happier about this whole thing."

"Happy!" his Mum said, "Load of rubbish, Susan, I won't feel happy, ever. You know why? Because they can't. They just can't. I mean, there's no answer to it, is there? All these things you need to have, they all cost money you know, and they don't have a clue!" She turned to Tracy.

"You're asking about the bloody computer for chrisssakes, and let me tell you, they cost Tracy, oh they cost a lot. So the whole thing is just out of the question, full stop. It's not a negotiation, it's not like there's something I don't understand about this that if you explained it to me I'd say yes all right then, it's just never, ever going to happen. End of story. You might as well go and play on the bloody computer, it would make as much difference as staying

134

here and talking to me. I have nothing else to say about any of this now, that really is it, it's just not happening."

Then George spoke, and what he said was something that Susan had read out to him from the instructions for the computer game months earlier. It was after she had told him the fairy story, she said the game begins with a saying. It had struck him at the time, and he had remembered it. It seemed to be the only thing he could say at that moment that made any sense.

"Love will find a way, you know?"

Chapter 11

Sometime Next Year

It was early, very early in the morning, George and Tracy lay side-by-side listening to the birds. George had slept fitfully through the night and now he lay still, not wanting to disturb her. She was so quiet lying next to him he had started to wonder if she was doing the same thing and not wanting to disturb him.

He could tell it was going to be another blazingly hot day, there was already some heat in the pale sunlight, stretching a thin line across the bottom of the bed.

He had known as soon as they walked in that this flat had to be the one they were going to get. It was the third they had seen, and this one felt lovely. The kitchen smelled fresh, it looked new and clean. The way the sunlight poured in through the bedroom window had made them both smile. The only thing he had not liked was the carpet in the front room. It was brown with an old-looking pattern of boxes with swirls inside. He thought it made the room look dark, and it was a bit like the carpet in his Mum's front room.

Tim had hung around in the hallway, as he had in all the flats, rattling the keys gently in his fingers and occasionally sighing. George sighed and looked over to the doorway where Tracy had slipped her warm, dry hand into his.

"This is it."

"Yeh, I know, you know? I mean I know."

Tracy had laughed as he stumbled over his words. He had realised, seeing the look she gave him, he always said you know about things that he knew. He had wondered then why he did that.

"Look at the light, imagine it, George." Tracy had let go of his hand and moved into the empty room, gesturing the shape of an imaginary bed.

"If we put the bed here, on a sunny day we'd have sunlight like this right across us. That would be great."

"Yeh, yeh it would."

He remembered that was when he realised they were going to be sharing a bed, the shape she had made was much bigger than his bed.

George smiled to himself at the memory and coughed quietly, to see if she heard. Tracy turned onto her side to face him. They shifted closer to each her. She stopped a few inches away, he could just feel the heat from her body on his. Tracy reached over and unbuttoned his shirt, slowly and carefully, George lay still and watched as her hand reached in and stroked his chest, over his shoulders. He pulled his arms out of his pyjama top, reached forward, and held the edge of her nightie at the tops of her legs. He was nervous and could feel his arms shaking as he pulled the delicate cloth up her body. She sat up and stretched her arms high, making it easy for him to take it off. He saw her pale skin revealed from the curtain of the cloth rising. George had never seen anything so beautiful, and a small noise escaped him. Tracy stayed sitting up and took his hand in hers, showed him exactly where and how she wanted him to touch her. He was grateful for her showing him like this, loving her more than he thought possible, she was so confident and sure.

As she let go of his hand he kept it there and let his fingers explore the way her nipple had tightened at his touch, it looked like something he could put in his mouth. As he did so she leaned into him and her hands found his pyjama bottoms and ventured inside. George moaned loudly at the feel of her hand where he had so often imagined it, and they fell back down to the bed entwined, enjoying the feels and tastes of each other's bodies.

Last night had been different, they had been nervous, George had been embarrassed about his erection and had tried to hide it, he had not been able to think about what Tracy might want, either from him or for him. They had kissed a lot, he had been so excited and nervous, he felt clumsy. George had not known what to do, Tracy seemed to be pushing against him in a way he had not understood, and he had pulled away so often she had eventually stopped and turned away. He wanted to try and talk to her, but had not been able to find the words and they had both fallen asleep without speaking.

This morning it felt right. She had been lying next to him all night, her shape and smell seemed so familiar now. Lying awake and worrying an hour ago George had realised that if Tracy truly loved him then she must love all of him . . . his erection as well. He decided she would need to be able to see him and they could work out what to do, but he should not pull away from her any more.

As they rolled together, Tracy put her arms right round him, pulling him on top of her, pressing her body right up against his like she had before. George realised that Tracy already knew what to do with him, and she fitted him inside her. This made her cry out and felt so amazing that he moaned with her. This was right, this was what they were supposed to do, George moved onto his elbows, his whole body on top of her and moved himself inside her. Tracy cried and clung onto him, but he knew it was all right, he knew in the way she pulled him to her that she wanted this in the same way he did, and that everything was going to be all right.

Afterwards the blood was a shock. They saw it together and George sat her down, putting his hand out to hers.

"Are you OK?"

"Yes, I think so, yes. I'm sore, but I liked it too, I want to try it again. I think this is all right, I think I remember something about this, it makes women bleed the first time? I think that's all right. Didn't Tim say something about that when he gave us the things?"

She could not remember properly, she had been too caught up in what the condoms were for and how to use them. A dread sinking feeling landed in her chest as she remembered the condoms, the full mystery of what they were really for became clear to her at the same time.

"George, we didn't use one of those things! That must be what they're for."

"Yes." He looked down, "What should we do?"

"I don't want to tell Tim we forgot. We didn't know, George, it would have made it all different again. I don't want to feel bad about it now. Let's just use one next time."

George grinned hugely and put his arms round her, holding her to him.

"OK, we won't say anything, we'll just put one on next time, and the next time, and the next time." She started laughing, realising why he had been holding her so tight. Yes, there were so many next times for them. It would be all right.

*   *   *

It had not mattered. None of it had mattered. All the shouting, all the objections, even the threat of legal action, none of it had mattered. George and Tracy had got on and got somewhere and moved in together. At first it had meant a lot, it had really mattered that people shouted and told them they could not do it. George had heard his Mum saying she would not let them, and believed her. Even Tim seemed to think that she meant it, and it meant that they would not be able to. Trying to convince everyone that they were just going to have to, that it did not matter if his Mum shouted, was the hardest thing George had ever done.

They had worked out how to talk to Oemor, and then none of the shouting had mattered any more. They simply knew, then, they were going to be together, they were going to do it, and nothing else mattered.

When George and Tracy had gone upstairs that evening, after telling his Mum about their engagement, they had sat down with Susan to watch her play the game. There had been some difficulties with getting it to play properly. Susan said Oemor had drowned and that she could not seem to get him back to the last saved game. She had always done it before. George had kept saying that he fell down to start with, and that was the bit he wanted Tracy to see . . . that was the bit he knew. Eventually Susan agreed to start it from the beginning, but that she had to help him in the fall.

George gazed at the screen as Oemor got out the c-cylinder, shook it and broke his fall. Susan and George jumped when he cried out as he wrenched his shoulders. He rolled smoothly down the tunnel, stood up, dusted himself off and said,

"What the hell is going on? I was in the water, now I'm back here again? And how come I know how to walk this time?"

George was still spluttering something about his dream and the c-cylinder when Oemor looked straight at him. He actually turned right to the screen and looked at George as he spoke. Susan and George leapt away from the screen and joystick, both crying out in surprise. They sat in a stunned silence as he got his gun, without Susan touching the joystick, and set off down the tunnel. She grabbed at the control and helped him on his way. She had felt before the effort it took him to force himself outside of her control, and getting that gun had not been easy for him.

As he jogged down to the cavern Susan and George realised that there were no giants, no rumbling in the caves. In fact the only noise was Oemor's breathing, heavily thumping in time with his footsteps, synchronised to Susan's heartbeat.

Tracy had no idea what was supposed to happen, so she simply sat on the bed grinning uncontrollably. The whole thing had hooked her straight away, having never been interested in computers, she had never seen anything like this. She thought it was amazing, like having a TV you could control.

Susan and George were getting worried, this was not playing out in the way that either of them knew the game. George had never heard him talk and never seen it without giants to shoot at before now. He was still realising that Oemor had used the same metal tube he had seen in his dream . . . the same dream that Susan had.

Susan had not seen the game right back at the beginning since she started to play, she was not sure if he would remember anything. It was clear something had permanently changed about the game. There were no more Nephillim, and no more saved games so she had no choice about going back to the cavern . . . what were they actually going to do?

"Where are they then?" Oemor's voice was clear and well controlled, he sounded just like a computer. His voice reminded Susan of the announcements at the railway station, each word pronounced separately, "What the hell is going on?"

At this point two things happened. Susan realised that if someone else worked the joystick, she might be able to get into, write in, and save the gaming journal without pausing the game. She asked George,

"Can you take control so I can try and talk back to him?"

As she spoke the red, horned, flying lion appeared at the other end of the cavern. She glanced round and saw George's face. His mouth was wide open, eyes staring in shock and excitement; he had clearly not seen the lion before. "Really, Sue? Are you sure . . . can I?"

"Course, George, . . . I'm here and I'm letting you, it's different to you sneaking in. Anyway, I want to try doing somethi . . . Oh my God!"

Susan had turned back to the screen to see that the lion was heading straight for Oemor. George was up, she had moved out of the way, and Oemor had already begun the arduous task of lifting his gun. George took the joystick in his hand and Oemor lurched from the shock. In that lurch, he managed to get the gun in place, and with George's careful, slow and precise help, he fired at the lion's face.

"Try shooting for the feet George."

As she said it Susan was typing it into the journal . . . she had opened it in the top corner of the screen.

"I can't make him lower it, Sue, I'm trying."

"OK, hang on . . . "

She saved the journal as it was, but kept the window open.

"Great, now he's doing it, hey . . . what did you do?"

As he spoke George's voice rose over the sound of the lion screaming. It was a shout of anger and fury, not like the Nephillim's shriek before death.

"It's not working, Sue, and it's still getting closer, can't we just shoot him all over? He might have another, you know, weak place we don't know about."

"Bloody hell, George, you're a genius . . . you start, I'll let him know."

George did just that, Susan wrote swiftly in the journal, pretty soon he was not fighting against Oemor, they were shooting together, and the smile that spread quietly across George's face was reflected in Oemor's on the screen in front of him.

"It's not making any difference, George. Now be careful because that tail has a really sharp blade in it. Last time this happened it didn't kill us, it just took all our weapons and picked us up and dragged us to a waterfall. I'm not sure what else we could do to try and survive."

"He could run away!" Tracy joined in, perched on the edge of the bed, avidly observing everything.

"We tried that before, it just flew right past us."

"Did he talk to it? Before, Sue, with me, you know . . . he never spoke."

"We just learned that, he kind of worked it out all by himself really, I mean, I helped a bit, but not much. Erm . . . yeh, he did try talking to it before, it didn't seem to make any difference."

"Maybe," Tracy leant forward, "He just has to get to the waterfall, then, maybe there's something there?"

"I guess you might be right, Tracy. I never really thought of that, it's not how the game has played out so far. There doesn't seem to be that much choice about it. What else are we gonna do huh?"

"Help!"

All the time they had been talking George had been fighting the lion as best he could, but to no avail, he had lost his gun, he had even tried the c-cylinder all by himself . . . it was still very much in his mind from the dream . . . but with no effect. The lion had bled and cried out, but it just stayed there. Oemor had been disarmed and wounded in the process but it had not killed him.

Susan was tapping away in the journal, and Tracy, after a moments pause, read out loud as Susan typed;

"I know this makes no sense dear love, but I do know what is happening to you all the time. I'll try and explain it later, but for now you just have to trust me that I do. It may still be that the lion is trying to show us something, it clearly is not going to put an end to us right now, why not let it take us to the waterfall, but then we need some time for a look round, maybe you could try talking to it or something. There's nothing to do once you're in the water, but maybe before then there might just be something, and what else can we do?"

As George heard this he helped Oemor to retract the c-cylinder, and as Susan saved the journal entry, there was that strange flicker, and Oemor put his arms down completely. The lion flew off towards the entrance he had come out from, and Oemor followed, teaching George how to make him jog with remarkable ease.

After a very short while, taking a couple of turnings Susan had never seen, they heard the waterfall ahead. Oemor turned round and again looked George straight in the eye.

"I want to get him to pick me up, I have an idea, we'll try it like last time eh?"

George jumped again at the voice and the eye contact, Susan gasped in delight and wonder.

"WOW. I wonder how he's worked that out."

"OK, George, what we did last time was to try and trick it. We walked away, because it was right in front of us, then we pretended to go the way it wanted and quickly ducked under it, and made a bolt for it. That's when it caught us."

George nodded, but as they approached the water and the noise started to deafen them, the lion flew straight upward and came down over Oemor's head. He clearly was not going to fall for any more tricks. Susan wondered if this too was a learning program. As the sharp talons grasped Oemor's tunic, he said,

"Come on then, reach up."

George immediately responded, and they reached up and grabbed on tight to the lion's paws He was taken over the waterfall, and the talons retracted to drop him once more into the mass of water and power below, but Oemor remained where he was, hanging there, holding on to the lion's fur. He had a good look round while the lion screamed and beat its wings, clearly trying to shake him off. His hold was a good one, and Oemor, Susan, Tracy and George looked carefully all around for something, anything, which might help him.

"There," Tracy saw it first, and pointed at the screen. Her finger hit the glass, which shocked her a little, she had been so lost in the game she had been pointing right into it. Her finger left a slight mark on the screen, which highlighted clearly for the other two, a shadow in the rock on the other side of the fall. It was not like the shimmering of hidden holes, but it might just be an entrance of some sort. Susan's fingers flew across the keyboard and saved as fast as she could.

"Let me this time, George, it's going to be tricky."

She pushed George away from the joystick and took hold.

"Ah, that's better" they could barely hear Oemor over the sound of the water, but it was clear he could feel a difference between George and Susan at the control.

Tracy moved over to the keyboard.

"I can do this bit. Not very fast, but I can type, OK?"

"Brilliant. Yeh, of course."

They were all so caught up in the game, Susan did not have time to register her surprise that Tracy could type.

"Tell him to swing towards the darker bit of rock, and then jump when we have enough momentum."

"Erm . . . OK, but I can't say it like that."

Susan started to work the controls and Tracy typed with three fingers, and saved the journal as she had watched Susan do it, and Oemor leapt from the lion's grip. He landed safely and flung himself forwards, scrabbling on the very edge of the wet rock. Sure enough it was an entrance, a very low one that he had to crawl into, but he did, he made it.

They all breathed a sigh of relief and weakly cheered as Oemor lay and got his breath back.

"Just look at his heartbeat!"

Susan pointed to a red bar at the bottom of the screen. As Oemor lay still it moved to the left and turned green. Eventually it was a small green streak which pulsed slightly in time with Susan's heartbeat for as long as she held the joystick. Oemor and Susan calmed down together before he set off crawling through the tunnel.

"This must be somewhere near the end, I can't imagine there would be much more than this now. There's usually like one big last trick before you can finish with these games."

As Oemor came to the end of the tunnel it opened out and they saw the bars of a cell, with a hunched figure, clearly chained to the wall.

"Oh, God . . . Susan? At last! It looks terrible in here. Are you OK?"

Oemor went to the bars, his face grimacing, and started to look round for a way to get in and unchain her. The figure sitting in the far corner raised her head weakly to face Oemor. All three of them gasped to see Susan's face, a slightly shaky three dimensional version of the school photo. She stood up and moved to the middle of the cell.

"Oemor my love? Is that you? Have you come to save me? Oemor my saviour set me free so I can once again return to my land and my dear father."

"Shit script huh," Susan was disappointed. She had spent so long with Oemor now, she had almost forgotten it was just a game, and it was not really her he was coming to rescue. Through the joystick she started to feel the effect on Oemor, and realised her own disappointment was a pale imitation.

Oemor was devastated. He was convinced that she had some force and power over him, which he could feel in him. It had been her idea to leap to the cave entrance, her voice in his head guiding him to see what he did not. How then could she greet him with these words? It did not make sense to him. Still his heart poured out to her, unstoppable as he searched for how to set her free.

"Yes, yes my dear love . . . love of my life, fire of my soul, you have been with me through all of this, you taught me how to talk, you have shown me the way, oh my dear sweet angel, I have so longed for you, I have ached every second we have been apart. Come, let me at least touch you, I will have you out of here, I know I will, but first let me touch even the tip of your finger, how I have longed for you and to gaze once more into your eyes."

The woman stayed where she was, standing facing him, looking forwards but not at him, unblinking . . . it was almost as though he had not spoken at all.

"Oemor my love? Is that you? Have you come to save me? Oemor my saviour set me free so I can once again return to my land and my dear father."

Oemor reached through the bars of the cell, but could not touch her. His heart was breaking in a state of anger and confusion. How could this be? It could not be true, he simply could not believe that this was his Susan, whose voice and thoughts and feelings he had carried with him. How could it be?

Tracy pointed to the padlock on the bars.

"Shame you don't have a knife or something to stick in there, I bet it would open."

Susan remained immobile; she was caught by the strength of Oemor's feelings. The devastating effect that this was having on him was flooding through her from the joystick. She could not figure out what to say to him . . . what should she let him know? How could she tell him none of it was real, he did not really exist, that the Susan that stood before him was nothing, and, come to that, he was also nothing but a piece of computer programming. She had not thought about what would happen at the end. Interrupting her thoughts came the tapping noise of Tracy writing in the journal, to try the lock with a knife.

"No! I mean, well . . . erm, OK, but hang on. We picked up a bunch of keys ages ago, I bet this is what they're for. Let me type it though OK?"

"Sorry."

"No, no it's OK, Tracy, I just . . . " She turned to face them, "I don't know if he should set her free, I mean, what would happen?"

"What do you mean?"

"He feels . . . well . . . it's breaking his heart, he has loved me so well and for so long, and then he's meeting this and it's not really me at all. I can't explain, here, you feel it."

Susan moved aside and let Tracy hold the joystick.

She was immediately hit by the strength of his emotions in a wave of shock and grief.

"Oh yes! I see . . . I mean I feel, now, yes, I know what you mean. Still what else can we do? George, you have to feel this, it's making me think about us, I want you to feel it."

As George took hold of the control he too was filled with the emotion from Oemor, at the same time he heard Tracy's words in his ear.

"It's making me think, George, what if this is what happens if we don't? What could happen to us now if we just go on and don't get married, like your Mum says and don't live together and don't have our child, George? It would feel like this. We can't not, we've spent so long asking if we can, whether we're going to be allowed to. We just have to, we can't go back to how we were. It would feel like this . . . it would be too much. We would spend all our time feeling this bad. We just have to do it, George, no matter what."

George let go of the joystick and turned to Tracy, knowing she was right, it made sense . . . where could they go from here but onwards. They could not have that terrible feeling of despair and loss they had both just experienced. He had no words, he simply nodded and kissed her gently before they both turned back to the game.

On the screen in front of them they watched as Susan took the control and guided Oemor to the keys; he opened the lock. The Susan character remained motionless until he rushed forwards and took her in his arms. He sobbed and she remained glazed, her arms reached automatically round his waist.

"Oemor my love? Is that you? Have you come to save me? Oemor my saviour set me free so I can once again return to my land and my dear father."

Oemor sobbed some more and clutched her to him, but there was no more response from her.

Tracy and George clung to each other, knowing what they had to do.

Susan wrote her final journal entry while Oemor stood in the cell and tried to talk to his beloved Susan.

"You're right Oemor, this is not really me. I don't exist in your world at all my love. You cannot rescue me, but you have helped me a lot . . . being loved by you has been an amazing experience. You do need to get her out of there though, she may not be me, but she is real . . . more real to you than I will ever be, and you cannot leave her there. I think that the lion is good, if you go out again with her, I think he will show you the way out this time. Get her out and it will all be all right I promise."

Susan clicked on save, took the joystick and guided Oemor, who had his arm around the woman. He almost fell straight into the waterfall. She had been right, as he stood there the lion swept down and picked him up once more by his tunic. Its huge wings beating strongly the lion lifted the two of them straight upward. They rose for a long time, and eventually the deep shaft opened out and they were lifted out of the Nephillim caves. As the lion flew back down the shaft leaving Oemor still holding the strange woman, the screen faded out, and in golden gothic writing they all turned to see the words,

"The End"

About the Author

Helen lives in Leeds, growing pumpkins and reading science fiction novels. Since writing this book she has written articles for Imagine, Community Living and Shout!

Helen has a long history working for Social Services in day services and with people who have high support needs. Helen ran a Sexuality and Sexual Health Support Project for learning disabilities services in Leeds.

Since joining Paradigm Helen has brought her down to earth and inspiring style to training and consultancy in person centred planning, modernising day services and working out creative, workable solutions with people who have high support needs.

Helen wrote her first story at the age of 7, and has been writing poems and short stories ever since. This is her first novel.

Dave Hingsburger

Dave Hingsburger is an internationally renowned behavioural therapist, originating from Canada. He is a consultant for schools, parents and agencies regarding problematic behaviour. For six years, he was the sex clinic co-ordinator at York Services in Ontario. Dave is also in private practice providing education and consultation for families, staff and agencies, advising around issues of challenging behaviour.

Being 'There'

by Dave Hingsburger

I have always been difficult to shoo away. Not being invited to the party is not the same as not attending. I first heard of her in whispered tones when all the other kids had been pushed outside to do what parents called, 'play'. Not I, I preferred lurking to playing. Still do. Unless the game is right. Her name was never said, aloud, Cousin Mattie. I never saw her, not even in a photograph. There must have been something mightily wrong with Cousin Mattie. After all they let Aunties Solvig and Vesta out at the 'in and out' state occasions of baby showers and funerals. So, why, when it was clear that something unholy had peed in our gene pool would we be whispering about Cousin Mattie. I guess what I really came to notice after having been oblivious for years was that Cousin Mattie was simply not there. She existed without existing. A being who would only occasionally make herself known by absence.

Then, suddenly, she was there. A woman now, sitting quietly drinking tea at the table in her mother's home. She appeared from nowhere. From the land of disability, from the province of difference. Poof. A new family member. Interested more in the lumps of sugar than in the lumps of flesh peering round the door at her. She fit like a magic key in a mystery chest. Suddenly. There.

I shouldn't be, but I am. Shocked. I knew he was there. It was my job to meet him and his teacher. I'm in my early twenties. I'm a consultant. How did that happen? The building was old. Really old. The school was in a very rural part of the region. Though the school I attended in Salmo was much different. I am reminded of it as I enter. Maybe it's the smell that schools have. Paste and sneakers. Chalk and stale air. Kirk wasn't there. All the kids in Salmo are typical. If you can call kids who show up with egg stuck to their shirts, typical. There must have been something mightily wrong with Kirk. They let in Debbie. Hell, they let me in. Other kids, damaged kids weren't even spoken of. We didn't have words for them.

Then, suddenly, he was there. A little boy with an awkward gait and frightened eyes. Kirk. The first kid with a disability mainstreamed into the school. I saw him negotiating the stairs and the stares. One at a time he stepped down them. Walking into frame. Stepping into real life. He existed. He had come from the place of lepers. A student named Kirk took his place in the unwritten history of the lost and the found. He fit like a prayer fits in God's hands. Suddenly. There.

Beans. Peas. Corn. Tomato Sauce. Noodles. I pulled groceries from the cart. Unaware that the world was totally changed. Money given. Change made. The bag was handed to me by a teenaged boy named Jackson. Who names their kids Jackson, I thought as I looked from badge to face. There should have been a thunder clap. Up until that day I never really noticed that he had never been here before. In any form. In any colour. But Jackson looked at me through eyes made with an extra chromosome. He smiled. I didn't. Maybe he saw hostility because he blinked, but indeed it was only shock. There must have been something mightily wrong with Jackson. I've been served by Raouls and by Helenas and by Susans if you can call being glared at 'served'. They got jobs. It never struck me as wrong during the time when Jackson wasn't around. Didn't exist.

Then, suddenly, he was there. Handing me my bag. Wishing me a good evening. Then going back to work setting up the next bag, grabbing the next can of asparagus. I kept glancing back wondering if he would disappear like hopes in adulthood. Vanish like incense into a stucco ceiling. He had come from shelter into sun. He acted like he didn't know that he had made the invisible visible. He fit like bread on top of the bag. Suddenly. There.

It started with an email. A request to review a book and maybe write an intro. Expected another good but dull book about 'residential setting' or 'behavioural challenges' or, God forbid, 'community integration'. I didn't know that I was about to read a work of fiction. And I shouldn't have been surprised. Helen Collins works for Paradigm in the UK and so do I. She full time. Me as a consultant/trainer. It's disability. All the time. Every moment. So when I turned the page and met George, I shouldn't have been shocked. But I was. Like Kirk stepped into view, like Jackson became 'seen', like Cousin Mattie drank tea – George took to the page like he ACTUALLY BELONGED THERE. He became real. He had flesh that responded to touch. He had a heartbeat in time with another. George. There must have been something mightily wrong with George. He and his ilk have been kept from fiction. Good God Hannibal Lector has FANS. Darth Vader stalks the universe in million selling books. Sure there've been caricatures like Forest Gump. But, George. A guy who gets by. A guy who wants love but fears his mother. A guy who has more obstacles placed in front of him than a video game hero and plods along towards his goal.

Suddenly he is here. And it's about time. He fits like a full stop at the end of a sentence.

Thanks, Helen, for George being suddenly there.

Paradigm is a consultancy and development agency working to promote better organisations, services and communities so that children and adults with learning difficulties can lead the lives they want. We work across the UK, and increasingly abroad, including Europe, USA and Australia. We are involved in a wide range of activities including conferences, training, project management, consultancy and publishing. This is our first foray into mainstream publishing. This book is part of our work that aims to encourage people to take an interest in everyone participating in community life. All children and adults with learning difficulties belong in our communities – we all have a responsibility to include everyone.

To find out more about the work of Paradigm visit our website at

www.paradigm-uk.org